5

'Why do you insult me so? Do you think I hold my honour, and that of my father, with so little respect that I would succumb easily to the desires of the flesh?'

Giles was out of the chair in a second. He watched her eyes widen as heat grew between them and within him until he burned from it.

He bent his head, forcing Fayth to tilt hers more. When he had moved his lips so close to hers that he could feel her breath against his skin, he paused.

'Desires of the flesh, lady?' he asked, dipping even closer. 'But there is much to commend those desires.'

The aching deep inside Fayth grew into a throbbing need she could not understand or ignore.

'Does your body not hunger for more, lady? Is there not an aching within to be touched in places you cannot speak of?'

Terri Brisbin is wife to one, mother of three, and dental hygienist to hundreds when not living the life of a glamorous romance author. She was born, raised and is still living in the southern New Jersey suburbs. Terri's love of history led her to write time-travel romances and historical romances set in Scotland and England. Readers are invited to visit her website for more information at www.terribrisbin.com, or contact her at PO Box 41, Berlin, NJ 08009-0041, USA.

Previous novels by the same author:

THE DUMONT BRIDE
LOVE AT FIRST STEP
 (short story in *The Christmas Visit*)
THE NORMAN'S BRIDE
THE COUNTESS BRIDE
THE EARL'S SECRET
TAMING THE HIGHLANDER
SURRENDER TO THE HIGHLANDER
POSSESSED BY THE HIGHLANDER
BLAME IT ON THE MISTLETOE
 (short story in *One Candlelit Christmas*)
THE MAID OF LORNE

and in Mills & Boon Historical *Undone* eBooks:

A NIGHT FOR HER PLEASURE*

*linked to *The Conqueror's Lady*

Look for Brice's story in
THE MERCENARY'S BRIDE
Coming soon in Mills & Boon® Historical

THE CONQUEROR'S LADY

Terri Brisbin

First published in Great Britain 2011
by Mills & Boon, an imprint of Harlequin (UK) Limited,
Large Print edition 2011
Eton House, 18-24 Paradise Road, Richmond, Surrey TW9 1SR

© Theresa S. Brisbin 2009

ISBN: 978 0 263 22296 8

11774498

Harlequin (UK) policy is to use papers that are natural, renewable and recyclable products and made from wood grown in sustainable forests. The logging and manufacturing process conform to the legal environmental regulations of the country of origin.

Printed and bound in Great Britain
by CPI Antony Rowe, Chippenham, Wiltshire

To Melissa Endlich,
my editor for the last seven years and
thirteen romances for Harlequin Historical.

Thanks for your support and advice
and help in making my books stronger
and in making me a better writer!
It's been a pleasure to work with you
and I wish you the best in
your new editorial position with Harlequin!

Prologue

Hastings, England
October 14, 1066

The Duke of Normandy surveyed the rolling fields before him and nodded to his commanders. Satisfaction, much like that of a well-fed cat, filled him as he realised that he would now be king of all he could see and more, much, much more. Anticipation surged through his veins and he smiled at the thought of seeing the faces of the Witan now, now that he'd defeated their *anointed* king and his forces. The clearing of several throats reminded him of the tasks still ahead. The battle for England, though advancing and in his control, was not a thing accomplished yet.

William turned and met the gazes of his commanders, who stood a short distance from him and his tent. These men and those who fought in their companies of foot soldiers, mounted knights and archers waited on his orders. And they waited for the rewards promised for a successful invasion. Already, the vultures of war were flocking to the battlefield, prepared to scavenge amongst the dead and dying.

'It will take days to clear the fields, my lord,' Father Obert, his clerk said.

'They—' William paused and nodded at the growing number of Norman, Breton, Poitevin, French and even Maine nobles approaching his tent '—do not seem to have the will to wait several days, Obert.'

William placed his goblet on the table and held out his hand for the parchment Obert had prepared for his review. A list of crucial English properties and fortifications along with the names of the men who would be the benefactors of his largesse. If he approved. Studying it, he recognised several names immediately, and others that were not the expected ones of his closest advisers or commanders.

'Who recommends such rewards to the nameless warriors here?' William suspected he knew, but before he gifted anyone with lands and titles he would understand the other motives in place.

'As usual, sire, the Bishop oversees that which is vital to your concerns.' Obert did not meet his gaze, but instead bowed his head.

Odo. Half brother and Bishop of Bayeux. He should have recognised the handiwork of the man in this.

'Ah, he is ever-vigilant on my behalf.' The words, true though tinged with a slight bit of mockery, drew a sharp snort from his clerk. Obert missed little in the intrigues that were court life, in Normandy and now here in England. It was part of his value. 'These will anger some who have laboured long on my behalf, risking lives and fortunes, only to see the choicest morsels go to others,' he observed.

William took note of three names and knew that even their fathers would object. Those objections, of course, would be couched in the politest terms to avoid mentioning the reason for their anger—they would want such lands to go to themselves or their legitimate offspring and not their bastards. His smile must have been a dangerous one for Obert backed away and waited without saying a word. Certainly not his usual response to such an open invitation to speak his mind.

'You must have some counsel to offer, good brother,' he said, encouraging, nay goading, him into saying the words he now held behind his teeth.

'My lord, the taking of those particular lands is in no way a certainty. They are probably the most dangerous that need to be claimed in your name. Mayhap, some will not even survive. 'Twould be a pity for some of your most loyal subjects to risk their heirs in such endeavours.'

William rose to his full height, nearly touching the top of his battlefield tent, and nodded. 'An interesting perspective, Obert,' he said, walking to the flap and lifting it higher, giving those outside the signal to approach. 'And a persuasive argument that will satisfy, at least for the immediate time, some of those who would be most vocal.'

'As you say, my lord.' Obert stepped to his side and they waited for the most noble, the richest and the most powerful of his supporters to enter. 'Why waste an heir on such a dangerous task when a perfectly good bastard will do?'

Another man would be dead on the ground for uttering such words to him. Indeed, many had lost much in doing such a thing in the past, but Obert spoke in understood irony as only one bastard could to another. Their own lives and positions had been based on such decisions. William caught sight of the bodies being piled all over the battlefield and nodded. His men were already calling this place *Senlac*, the blood lake. And there would be much more blood spilled before he controlled the length and breadth of England.

It did not matter to the ground beneath him if the blood soaking into it was noble or not. It did not matter to the clay if the man leaking his life held a title or even a name. It did not matter to the earth at his feet if his cause was right or wrong.

And it did not matter to him, William, Duke of Normandy, the Bastard, and now the Conqueror. Only success mattered now and, if those on Odo's list had much to gain and little to lose, so be it. He crossed his arms over his chest and nodded to Obert, who began to read out the declarations.

In war, success mattered, blood did not.

Chapter One

'Finish the words and you will be a widow before you are a wife,' Giles Fitzhenry, knighted warrior of William the Conqueror, promised in a harsh whisper.

The blood from the gash above his eye flowed down his face and dripped on the lady's shoulder, but still he did not relent in his crushing hold. It would take but a moment's pressure to crush her throat and he swore to himself and then aloud that he would do it if she spoke the words of the vow. Giles turned to face the now-quieting crowd in the small chapel and revealed the dagger he aimed at her ribs, another assurance that the lady would die if anyone tried to intervene.

His intended moved with him, gripping his hand as though she could stop him. Lady Fayth of Taerford should have thought about the re-percussions of her actions before he arrived. Before his men and hers had been killed in the battle for the keep…and for possession of her. Giles nodded to Roger and his man held his sword to the neck of the lady's comrade in this crime, waiting for her response.

'The keep and lands are mine now, lady, as are you. Your choice of words will simply bring his death more slowly or more swiftly.' Giles watched as the woman in his arms exchanged glances with the man held a few yards away.

He felt her body relent before she spoke the words of surrender. Trying with all his deter-mination to ignore the soft, womanly curves beneath his arm, he lessened his grip a tiny bit and lowered the dagger to give her the oppor-tunity to make the choice. 'Do you take him to husband instead of me?' he asked aloud.

'I do not,' she whispered hoarsely into the deathly silence that had covered the room.

With her capitulation, his men surrounded her people and began to force them from the chapel. Without letting go, he nodded at his second-in-command and then at the man who she had chosen as husband. 'Kill him.'

The priest protested loudly, but his men ignored the old man and prepared to follow Giles's orders. It was her quiet voice that stopped him.

'My lord,' she began, trying to face him in spite of his grasp. Her movement simply made his blood drip and smear more over her cloak. It wasn't until he lessened his grip on her that she could speak louder.

'I beg you, my lord. He is not to blame. Truly. Mercy, my lord. Mercy.' She leaned her head back, offering herself as a sacrifice to his anger.

He would tell himself later that it was his need to put an end to the bloodshed that made him relent. He would tell himself that he had never planned to kill the man cajoled or ensorcelled by his betrothed into this foolhardy plan to interfere with his rights to her and the land. But Giles only knew that at the moment when his gaze met hers he wanted to grant her whatever she asked of him. He let out his breath and nodded.

'Take him and his men to the edge of *my lands* and release them,' he said in a loud voice. 'And if, from this time forward, they step back onto *my lands* or try to contact *my wife*, kill them without hesitation.'

After Roger dragged his prisoner from the chapel, Giles released his hold on her. She gasped for breath as he pushed her to another of his men. There was much to do and he needed her out of his way.

'Find a place and secure the lady.'

Reaching up to touch her throat, she turned as though she would speak, but said nothing. His bloody handprint marred her neck and he knew that the armour gauntlets he wore would leave bruises on her fair skin where he'd held her. Any measure of sympathy he began to feel for her was extinguished when he saw that two of his men lay dead in the back of the chapel.

Giles met her gaze once more and the hatred burning there in her dark green eyes said more than her words would have or could have. Giles smiled grimly at her, accepting the challenge made silently.

'Nothing is to happen to her, except by my word or by my hand,' he called out.

'Aye, my lord,' his soldier answered as he dragged Fayth from his presence.

After surveying the chapel and making certain that his dead and wounded were cared for, Giles strode to the keep to see what his new home looked like.

She smelled the metallic odour of his blood on her and felt its stickiness on her skin where his gauntleted hand had clutched her. It was as though he had marked his possession of her where all could see it. Fayth's throat burned and her chest ached from his crushing hold. As his men dragged her across the yard, she saw Edmund and his men being chained together. Pulling against her guard, she managed to come to a stop, but she feared the cost of calling out to Edmund. When their captors finished chaining them, they were hauled across the yard and out of the gate.

Would she ever see him again? Would her new lord and master keep his word and see them released? Fayth fought back tears at the thought of never seeing her childhood friend alive again. At least she'd been able to save his life, but now that everyone who had protected her was gone, she alone was left to face this invasion.

The clamouring at her side caught her attention and Fayth looked on in horror as her people, the servants and villeins of the keep, were herded into the yard that usually held their horses. Men, women, children. Sir Giles's men were systematically going building by building and forcing all of her people out to the yard where they were thrown with the others.

Did he mean to kill them all? They called out to her, fear in their voices and terror in their gazes. What could she do now for she was a prisoner herself?

When one of the Norman soldiers tossed the cook's young daughter to the ground, she could no longer stand by silently. With a strength that surprised her, she pushed off the grasp of her guard and ran to young Ardith, knocking the warrior away from her. Helping the girl to her feet and urging her to run, Fayth turned back just as her guard caught up with her and as Ardith's attacker regained his feet.

Cursing in Norman French, words too gruff

and too fast for her to comprehend, the man grabbed her by the cloak she wore and pulled her to face him. The anger flared in his eyes at being interrupted in what he must have thought was his due as the conqueror. He raised his fisted hand and swung it at her. She tried to lean away to avoid the blow, but his hold was too strong.

Pain exploded in her head and then there was nothing but darkness.

He watched the chaos of the yard from the open window in the chamber he claimed as his own. The large room boasted a hearth built into the wall, a privy closet and this window that overlooked the yard and gate. Below him, most of the people of Taerford Keep were collected in an enclosure with a few stragglers being taken there now. His men controlled the gate and the roads leading to it.

They'd fought their way from Hastings, along the roads past London and out to the west, into Harold's country. William urged his haste in following a few who escaped the battlefield and ran to organise resistance to the duke's lawful control of England. Days became almost a week as they faced battle after battle and finally made their way to his promised fief.

In spite of sending word ahead of his claim and his approach, the lady and those who conspired with her had nearly completed their hasty marriage when Giles managed to take control of the keep. He smiled grimly.

Now, it was his.

The building was not very large, but would suit him. It contained three floors with several private chambers and a separate kitchen building. The keep, kitchen, chapel and several other shops were enclosed by the wall. It was not large, but it pleased him and would offer protection until he could replace the wood with stone as William had ordered.

Pushing the mail coif off his head, Giles looked for something to staunch the bleeding from his wound and found a small linen kerchief on the bed. Pressing it against the deep gash, he walked back to the window to watch his orders being carried out. Unfortunately, things were not going as he had instructed.

The newest soldier in his company had some

young girl in his grasp, his intent obvious even from this distance. Damn him! Giles had made it clear that such attacks were unacceptable, but Stephen had thrown control away during the battle and now the girl was his next target. Running from the chamber and down the stairs, Giles reached the yard in time to see the lady Fayth intervene.

Before Giles could shout an order, Stephen reached out and grabbed Fayth, lifting her from her feet. Giles called for him to stop, but the noise in the yard prevented anyone from hearing it. As he took off running towards them Stephen hit Fayth with enough force that the lady fell to the ground unconscious. Without stopping, Giles ploughed into the soldier and took him to the ground. Heedless of those watching, he pummelled him until he himself was pulled away.

'Andre!' he called to a guard. 'Carry the lady to my chambers. Henri, find her servant or a healer and see to her care. And,' he added, wiping his mouth of the blood that flowed freely once more, 'do not leave her side.' He turned to face Stephen, who still lay on the ground at his feet. 'Your disobedience and lack of control have ever been your weakness,' he accused. 'You have been warned about this and you have not heeded my words.'

Giles ordered him lifted, stripped to the waist and tied to the fence. The yard was eerily silent now as all watched their new lord discipline one of his own. He would rather not have carried this out now, but a prompt response to disobedience by any of his men was necessary, especially in a time of war. He tugged off the gauntlets and accepted the whip from his second-in-command. Giles did not do this lightly, for he'd felt the lash bite his skin, but he'd learned the hard lesson it taught quickly and had rarely faced discipline again.

Walking to the fence, he looked at those now held in the enclosure and at his men. 'For disobedience of my standing orders, the punishment is ten lashes. Call them, Thierry.'

Giles unwrapped the length of leather and flicked it into the air. The tip cracked loudly and many of those around him flinched, though no target was touched. He took several paces back and then applied the punishment he had decreed. Thierry counted out the number so that all could hear. Although Stephen hissed with each lash, he kept himself from crying out or bucking. At ten, Giles took a deep breath and paused.

'And for laying hands on the lady Fayth, ten more.'

His words surprised all who watched for he heard the gasps at his declaration. Giles lifted his arm again and again until the strokes numbered ten. Stephen's control had waned and he moaned at each bite of the whip. No one moved until Giles nodded his consent.

'Remove him and leave him there. When we finish the work we have ahead of us, then someone can see to his wounds.'

He met his men's gazes then before turning around and walking away. Two of his men removed Stephen and went back to the tasks he had assigned before the incident had stopped them, now a man short due to the stupidity and lust of one of their own.

Giles looked around and noticed the sun was not even at its highest point in the sky yet. Sweat and blood now poured down from his head, under his mail and tunic. He had been fighting since just after dawn and he was tired. Once he was certain that his men had control over the yard and the inhabitants, he motioned to Thierry to follow him into the keep.

The days of fighting his way across England were catching up with him and he wanted nothing so much as a secure home, a hot bath and a meal to fill his belly. From the looks of the keep and the turmoil still moving through it, Giles knew that he would not be getting his wishes fulfilled this day.

And he still had to deal with his new wife-to-be.

Her first attempt to open her eyes met with a head-shattering pain, so Fayth lay very still and waited until the urge to vomit quieted. She listened without moving as someone, or some ones, shuffled about the chamber. She was tempted to try again, but the waves of pain pulsing through her skull warned her not to.

'My lady?' The whispered words came from a familiar voice, but she could not recognise it so at the moment. 'My lady?'

Fayth swallowed and then again, but she could not speak. Her head felt as though it would shatter if she tried to answer, but the blasted woman, whoever she was, was relentless.

'You must wake up, my lady. He is coming.'

Lifting her hands, Fayth slid her fingers over her forehead and scalp until she found the lump. Gliding softly over it, she knew the source of the pain. With her arm shielding her eyes from the light pouring into the chamber, she forced them open.

It was Ardith. The young girl's tear-streaked face filled with terror as she turned to the door and then back to her. When the door opened, Ardith jumped to her feet and backed away, stopping only when her body hit the wall of the chamber. Fayth watched her as long as she could, but the waves of dizziness made it impossible after a few moments.

'You were told to care for her wound. Why is she still covered in blood?'

The words, in halting English, echoed in the room, making Fayth's stomach clench. Ardith was terrified into silence and could only offer a soft sobbing sound at the question. If Fayth could, she would intervene. But the pain and dizziness made it a thing she could not accomplish. She finally found her tongue.

'She is not used to such duties,' she whispered, hoping that the effort was enough. It made the terrible pain increase and made her stomach begin to heave.

Luckily the girl could recognise what was about to happen. Ardith grabbed a pail from the corner and held it out just as Fayth began to retch. By the end of it, she had not the strength to lift her head from the bucket and would have stayed in that humiliating position had not a strong pair of hands lifted her up and guided her back to the pillow.

'Get rid of that now!' he commanded.

It did not have the effect he wanted, for Ardith simply cowered farther into the corner, shaking so badly that she nearly dropped the offensive bucket to the floor. Fayth could only watch as the warrior approached and cursed in Norman French at the girl. Then the commotion outside the door stopped him and Emma entered, carrying a pail and some linens.

'My lord,' she said, curtsying before him. 'You

are terrifying her—' Emma stepped around him and held out her hand to Ardith '—as are your men.'

Watching was all Fayth could do as her old serving maid placed the things she had brought in on the table, took the bucket from Ardith's shaking grasp, and walked with it, past the astonished lord, to the door. Pulling it open, she pushed it into the hands of one of the soldiers there and ordered him away with it. Only the lord's loud laughter allowed the man to move.

'You do not seem terrified, old woman. What is your name?'

'Emma is old, my lord. Please…' Fayth whispered, trying to lean her head up to stop the wrath she knew would follow.

'Old enough to have wiped your arse when you were but a babe-in-arms, my lord,' Emma retorted without a speck of hesitation or the proper respect needed in this situation.

Worse, she put her hands on her hips, almost daring him to take some action against her. Dear God! He would kill her for such impertinence. It was the humour that shocked her again.

''Twould appear so, from your age and mine.' He laughed for a moment as he glanced back at the man closest to him. He made a comment in Norman that was too mumbled and too fast for her to understand and then sobered. 'Do not mistake amusement as permission for your boldness to continue, woman.'

This time, Emma did back down and lower her gaze. Although she was used to her maid's ways, everything now was different and Fayth had no way of knowing where offence would be taken, even from innocent words or gestures. Not that Emma was innocent…

'Lady Fayth, join me in the hall as soon as you are able,' he ordered in English now as he glared at her. 'There are matters to be handled and they must be handled as quickly as possible.'

'But, my lord—' Emma began.

With a wave of his hand and a dark look at each of them, he stopped any arguments. 'In the hall. Get her ready.'

Wisely, Emma only nodded and moved to the table to begin her duties. The new lord of Taerford walked out of the room, giving orders as he went until only silence remained in the chamber. When the door closed and they were alone, Emma leaned towards her and motioned for Ardith to move closer.

'I thought he would strike you down, Emma. You must not anger him,' Fayth urged. But the words were barely out before the servant shook her head in disagreement.

'My lady, this new lord respects only strength.' Emma reached over and slid her arm behind Fayth's shoulders, readying her for what Fayth knew would be a horrible experience. 'You must prepare yourself now and meet his strength with your own. Be the daughter your father knew you would be.'

Fayth wished that Emma's confidence were enough to convince her of the truth of her words, but the shocking events of this day were too fresh to allow her to hide in ignorance. And his words warned of more dire changes to her life and her people. Did Edmund yet survive? Could he rally his supporters, as he'd claimed, to take England back?

She was so caught up in her thoughts that Emma's sudden movement bringing her up to sit surprised her. The pain from such a grievous head injury should not have. It was several hours later that she was ready to go to the hall. Her legs trembled until Emma was forced to call two guards to her side. Better to be assisted down the steep stairway than to end up at the bottom of it in a heap, she advised.

Fayth concentrated only on putting one foot in front of the other and did not see the new lord until she stood before him. At his frown, his men let go of their hold and stepped back. Just when she thought she would fall over from the throbbing in her head, Fayth caught sight of something new on the Norman knight. Her father's signet ring, a thing he would never remove in life, hung on a chain around the new lord's neck.

Her father's ring.

Fayth looked up and met his gaze. A satisfied look rested on his face, confirming without words his position and his rights here.

Her father was truly dead and this man owned everything that was once his.

The truth sank into her, but she could not accept it. Fayth reached out to take the ring from him. He grabbed her hand just as she grasped it in hers and squeezed it hard.

'It is mine now. As are this keep, and you. King William has named me Baron of Taerford to rule over all the lands that Bertram ruled and more.'

In spite of her agreement with Emma about presenting her strength to him, Fayth lost control in that moment. The hall and the keep began to spin and she gave herself up to the pain in her head and now in her heart.

Her father was dead.

Chapter Two

Three days passed by before she regained her wits and Fayth did not see her captor during that time. At the least, she did not think so, but a few confused memories of a deep voice rousing her from sleep several times that first night told her to suspect otherwise. Emma spoke of a leech's directions not to let her sleep too long a time or her mind would be for ever muddled. The clarity gained from the still-throbbing pain in her head assured her she was not so.

Fearing that any moment could see her dragged to the hall and married to the Norman knight kept her from ever truly letting her guard down. Nay, not Norman, though he fought for the Bastard. She rubbed at the growing ache in her forehead. He hailed from Brittany, Emma had informed her, along with the men who fought at his side. His place of origin gave her no relief from worry, for William the Bastard had gathered men from all parts of the continent to fight for him and his illegal campaign to gain control over her country.

As he had gained control over her keep.

His first orders found her moved into her father's chambers while the usurper took hers. And though the door remained impassable for her, for she was stopped by the guards each time she tried to leave, Emma moved freely through the keep and grounds. Ardith stayed mostly at Fayth's side, fearing further attention from the soldier who'd attacked her three days before. From what Emma had learned, this Giles le Breton had an iron grip over her home now. He'd replaced the soldiers her father had left behind with his own, he'd placed his men to oversee every aspect of the workings of her keep and people and had done it without any regard for her.

Fayth squinted then, as the soreness in her head made it impossible to concentrate on her stitches. Tossing the gown she was repairing into the basket at her feet, she tilted her head one way and then another, trying to ease the ache there.

'Ardith,' she said, beckoning the girl to her side. 'Can you loosen these braids? The weight of them is pulling too much.'

Fayth turned herself in her chair, allowing Ardith to get closer. Once the girl let down the twist of braids some of the pain eased. Fayth closed her eyes, relaxing her head and letting her chin fall to her chest. Her hair hung loosely now around her shoulders and she waited to see if the pain would pass.

The silence surrounded her for a few minutes until Ardith's nervous breathing drew her attention. As she raised her head her gaze met that of her captor as he stared at her from his place inside the door. She hadn't heard the door open, but it was apparent he'd been there for several minutes.

'Sir Giles,' she said, rising to stand yet refusing to call him by another title he now claimed. 'I did not hear you enter.'

Fayth motioned to Ardith to arrange her hair once more. It might be her chambers, but it was not proper, with a man present, to be so undone. Ardith hurried in her attentions and Fayth winced against the pulling as the girl gathered her hair into one long braid and re-placed the veil on top of it. Once her hair was covered, she faced him and nodded.

'Are you well, lady?' he asked, his deep voice accented by the language of his own country.

'Other than…' she began, and then realised that any complaints would sound trite when compared with those her people could offer.

'Your head?' he asked, nodding in her direc-tion. 'Does it still pain you?' He stepped closer, handing the helm tucked under his arm to one of his men.

'It is improving,' was all she would offer. Emma's words about appearing strong before him echoed in her thoughts and, though he frightened her to her core, she was now the only one left who could protect her people. They must be uppermost in her priorities now.

Now that her father was gone.

Fayth glanced down and saw the ring he still wore, dangling there as a sign to everyone of her father's death and this man's new rule.

He frowned as she looked up at his face. Then

his gaze and his mouth hardened. The tension in the chamber grew until one of his men whispered something under his breath to him and Giles nodded as though reminded of some task.

'Now that it is safe to move about the keep and village, I thought you might like a respite from your stay here,' he said, his voice neither welcoming nor comforting. Another whisper from his man and he said, 'I know you worry about your people, *our* people, and I would have you be at ease over their condition now that I have—' he paused, searching for a word '—arrived.'

Tempted in spite of her resolve to be wary of this stranger, she nodded. 'I would like that, sir.'

He motioned the others out of the chamber ahead of them and then held out his arm to her. With his armour in place, it was clear he did not yet feel safe in her keep. That thought made her smile for the first time in many days. As she lifted her arm and placed her hand on his she felt a sense of anticipation unknown to her since learning of her father's death.

Although this warrior carried her father's ring, she had no way of knowing the part he had played in his death. Chances were, though, from the way he had seized control of her lands with his king's permission, he had been involved. Now, regardless of the origin of their lives, their destinies were entwined and she needed to find her place in this new world his arrival had wrought.

They stopped just outside her door and he turned back, speaking to her of Emma and Ardith. 'The old one and the girl have the freedom of the keep and village now, lady. They need worry not over their safety.'

Without saying so, he told her that the man who had tried to rape her servant and had knocked her unconscious was under control. Had he been executed, then? Disobedience in time of war could be punished with death, she knew. Was this man such a hard commander that he would do that? She stopped then and faced him.

'Why? Is that man dead?' she asked.

'Nay, not dead,' he answered before tugging her along at his side. 'Stephen has learned not to disobey my orders.'

She shivered at the coldness of his words and

the inherent threat as she moved down the stairs to the main floor. Then out into the yard they walked until she stood in nearly the exact spot where the incident with Ardith had occurred.

He stopped and Fayth took a few moments to catch her breath. Even feeling well she would have difficulty matching his long strides, but feeling as she did, only his arm pulling her along had kept them together. Now, she inhaled deeply, enjoying the scents of soil and air and the recent rain. Harvest had passed even while her father rode the length of England following their king and it had been a meagre one.

Both Emma and Ardith followed them, along with three of the knight's men. Once she could breathe more easily, he led her to one of the smaller yards where he'd penned her people the day of the attack. The people were gone and the enclosure held cattle once more, though fewer than before.

Fayth lifted her hand to shield her eyes from the sun and peered to the limits of the yard. There along the perimeter of the wall, his soldiers now paced. As she moved her gaze to the farthest part of the yard his soldiers worked alongside some of her men, carrying logs that would be hewn into boards for repairs to the walls and the other buildings.

'Part of the blacksmith's cottage burned during the battle. They rebuild it now,' he offered, pointing in the other direction where men worked on the small croft that was attached to the smithy.

Everywhere she looked, the situation was the same. Though outnumbered now because so many had fled at first sight of the invader's forces, her people wore no prisoner's chains. Indeed, many seemed to be doing their usual duties in spite of a new lord in control of the lands. Suddenly, as many saw her there, they stopped their work and stared at her. Before she understood what was happening, Sir Giles clasped her hand in his larger one and held it high into the air.

'As I told you,' he called out in a voice loud enough to travel across the open space to the walls, 'your lady is alive and well.'

Fayth could not help her response, for her people called out her name, and it resonated around the yard, warming her heart and giving her pride at their concern for her well-being.

'You did this to show them you have not killed me?' she asked. She turned to face him and saw amusement in his features. His blue eyes, so dark and intense, now lit with some humour.

'I have not killed you, yet, *demoiselle,*' he answered in a voice meant only for her ears. Leaning in close to her, he whispered, 'If I discover you still work to betray me, it may yet happen.'

The shiver of fear tore through her at his words and tone. She wanted to believe he was speaking in jest, but there was a thread of steely resolution and something else, something dangerous, in his voice and she did not doubt for a moment that her life was in peril should he choose it to be so. Leaning away, but not able to free her hand from his grasp, she straightened her shoulders and met his gaze.

'You would not find it to be an easy task, sir,' she said, watching and waiting for his response to her challenge.

He said something to the man closest to them

and then smiled at her. 'Ah, *demoiselle*. You are correct—it would be no easy thing.'

He laughed then and lowered their hands, allowing hers to drop to her side. She clasped hers together in front of her and waited. 'Come, this way, if you please.'

She allowed his stride to take him ahead of her and took advantage of the distance to study this warrior. He was tall, more than six feet in height, and his build declared his strength. Though most of him was covered in mail and armour, she did not doubt that he was as fit and muscular under all of his protection as he appeared to be.

He wore his pale brown hair longer than the Norman custom, yet shorter than the English way. No beard grew so there was no hiding the sharp angles of his face and his strong chin. His eyes, though blue, darkened when he was vexed as she'd seen already, but stayed a paler shade when no mood changed them. Fayth would never declare him to be a handsome man, yet his masculine features were powerful and unforgettable.

He stopped and waited for her to catch up. She

noticed then, for she'd been too busy staring at his face before, that they'd reached the chapel. The low stone building had been the scene of the horrific fight that had ended in her capture and Edmund's near-murder. Giles Fitzhenry opened the wooden door and waited for her to enter.

It took all her resolve to do so, for she imagined she could hear the screams of the injured men and smell the spilled blood from the wounded. Her own neck burned as she remembered his gauntleted grasp around her throat, choking the air from her, and threatening her death.

'Come,' was his only word to her as he walked ahead, down the aisle where the benches had been replaced and the blood washed away.

It was Emma who stood then at her back and urged her forward to follow the knight. Two of the knight's men remained behind her, standing on either side of the doors and watching her through the slits of their helmets. Another shiver tore its path down her spine and back to her head, sending tremors through every part of her. She followed his footsteps up the centre aisle and found Father Henry standing before the altar. From his stern expression, he wanted to be present no more than she did. Still they both did as the Breton knight ordered.

A few moments passed after she stopped at his side and Fayth found her nervousness growing within her. When he reached out and took her hand in his now-bare hands, the truth of it struck her—they would marry here and now.

Surely not?

From his intense gaze, she knew they would indeed.

'Lady, I will not go forth with this ceremony unless you give your free consent here,' Father Henry said with a bravado she thought impossible.

Had he given Fayth an escape then, with his words? If she did not consent, could this man lay no claim to her lands or her person? Without looking at Giles Fitzhenry, she began to object when he squeezed her hand so hard she gasped. Turning to him, she followed his nod to the back of the church.

Her servants and villeins stood watching, surrounded by his warriors dressed for battle. Herded in like the cattle they tended, they bunched together watching the unfolding drama before them. They could not see what she could—the weapons held at the ready were aimed at them and not held for their defence. Facing the knight, she searched his face for his true intentions.

'You would harm innocent servants, then?' she asked.

'Nay, lady. Your actions determine their safety. Fulfil your duty as their lady and all will be well.'

'If I do not give my consent, what then?' She held her breath waiting for his inevitable answer.

'I will still hold these lands for my king, but I will need a new wife.' Tempted to believe he jested with her, she glanced at his face and saw the truth there. 'My duke has requested,' he explained, '*requested,* that his men take the daughters of the land we gained to wife. If there is no daughter, we may seek wives where we may.'

'So you would execute me here in God's

House, sir? With my people looking on at your murderous act?'

She pulled her hand free of his grasp and crossed her arms over her chest, challenging him with every fibre of her being. He leaned in close, so close that she could feel his breath against her neck. Shivers of another kind pulsed through her at his nearness and the sudden heat he caused.

'There is no reason to execute you, for a woman as lovely as you has several uses. Several that come to mind immediately,' he repeated, stepping nearer and lifting her chin so she had to meet his gaze. His eyes took on a different expression then, heated and filled with desire, and she knew she would not like his words before he spoke them. 'Perhaps I will strip you of your position as lady here and keep you instead as my leman while I search out a new wife.'

If he was trying to intimidate her, he'd been successful, for she could see no way out of this predicament and her fears threatened to overwhelm her. In order to succeed in her own quest, to keep her people safe until they could be freed from Norman control, she needed to stay alive and that meant acquiescing to his demands. Emma's nervous whispers from behind her drew her attentions.

'Please, lady, do as he asks,' she begged quietly, so quietly that only the three of them heard it.

'Aye, lady, do you do as I ask or not?' he said in a soft and misleading tone. 'Father Henry has asked if you consent to our exchanging vows.' He raised his voice now as he stepped back, releasing her. 'Do you, Lady Fayth?'

He held out his hand in a gesture she knew was to increase the pressure on her and to make it impossible to answer any other way than the one he wanted. The silence grew and held them all motionless as they waited on her word. Glancing at Giles, she noticed the hint of a smile at the corners of his mouth and she wanted more than anything to wipe it from his face, though she dared not do so.

Everything she'd lived for was at stake here. At least with Edmund there had been a mutual affection and a common cause between them. She would gain a stranger as husband now; her people would gain a foreign lord who had conquered their lands. A man with no experience other than gaining such prizes with his powerful sword. He moved his fingers ever so slightly to remind her that he, nay they, waited for her response.

As though she had any choice at all?

Edmund was probably still shackled somewhere close by and not able to gather and bring some strong army to her rescue. Her father's friends and allies lay dead and broken on some distant field of battle. No one could help her.

Taking in a deep breath and releasing it slowly, she did the only thing she could do—she placed her hand in his and walked at his side towards the altar and Father Henry.

Nothing after that mattered, not the words or the gestures, not the cheering of her people or of his men, not the solicitous way her new husband guided her back to the keep. She sat at his side and thought she remembered him feeding her from their shared trencher and drinking mead from a shared cup, but it all passed her by in a haze. If she responded to questions or spoke at all, she could not later say. All she could comprehend was that her life was no longer her own. She now belonged to a man who might have killed her father.

It was not until the door of her chambers closed behind them, leaving her alone with a man not of her family for the first time in her life, that she realised the extent of the changes she faced. Unsure of what to do or what to say, she was saved by his words.

'I did not want blood to be shed today because your people tried to defend you from me. I lured you to the chapel in a way I thought would prevent that.' Though he spoke softly, the expression in his eyes now burned with manly desires.

'So your threats to have me killed or to take me as your whore were…?' she asked, trying to sort through her confusion and surprise.

She watched silently then as he walked to the table set in the middle of the room and poured wine from a pitcher into two cups. He brought one to her and waited for her to drink from it.

'Provocations only, meant to divert your attention from my true intentions.' He smiled then, one that resembled a genuine one. 'And they seemed to work.'

Glancing at the ring that now encircled her finger, proclaiming her position as his wife, she nodded. Nervousness poured through her at the thought that she was completely at his mercy. Mercy she could not be certain even existed. She swallowed all the wine he'd poured for her.

'There are less offensive ways to distract me, sir,' she said before correcting her error. 'My lord.'

That fact had seeped into her mind even as she tried to reject it. The marriage contract proclaimed him Lord Giles Fitzhenry, Baron of Taerford. Grief clouded her thoughts then, making it difficult to even breathe at the constant reminders of her father's death. She could not meet his gaze and witness the joy he must feel at his elevation to such an honourable, ancient title.

Still she was her father's daughter and would bear whatever was necessary to keep their people safe through the turbulent and violent times ahead of them. She met his gaze then, not knowing what to expect from this new lord.

'I will try to remember that in the future,' he said.

He drank deeply from his cup and placed it back on the table. Was it time then to…consummate their vows? Fayth looked to the empty cup wishing that she'd left some to strengthen her resolve to carry through the act ahead of her.

Expecting his move towards her, she tried to calm her apprehension at the forced intimacy they would share. Giles walked slowly towards her and took the goblet from her shaking hands. Fayth looked up at him, standing so close she could feel the heat of him, and waited for him to take the first step.

The touch of his lips on hers shocked her in its gentleness. He moved his mouth over hers, once, twice and then again, before he settled it firmly there. Though he touched her in no other way than this joining of their mouths, she closed her eyes and prepared herself for his next move.

She was still standing there when he stepped away, turned and walked to the door, facing her then with his hand on the latch.

'I bid you a good night's rest, lady,' he said, nodding to her.

Fayth paused, not knowing what words to say. As she touched her fingers to her tingling lips a fear unlike any before filled her. That kiss was far gentler than she ever expected, but the thought of giving herself to a man, a warrior now called husband and lord, was more terrifying now that she faced the act itself.

'Sir,' she said, shaking her head and not understanding his intentions again. 'My lord, will you not…?'

'No.' He shook his head in reply. 'Until I know you do not carry your lover's child in your belly, we will not…' He imitated her hesitation and threw a glance and a nod across the chamber at the bed.

Fayth could not stop her jaw from dropping at that pronouncement. They would not? He would not? The terror that threatened her moments ago fled and anger replaced it.

'I carry no child!'

'Do you confess that he was your lover, then?'

She strode across the room and met his disrespectful gaze. 'I am an honourable woman, sir.

How dare you?' She raised her hand to strike him in answer to such an insult.

He caught it easily and she waited, expecting him to strike back for such behaviour. Instead his eyes took on a calm appearance and he shook his head at her.

'You would give your body and self to one of your father's men, elevate him to such a lofty position and get nothing in return?' He crossed his arms over his chest. 'A man does not risk his life for nothing more than tupping a woman. What promises did Edmund make to you in exchange for your marriage vow?'

'You again insult me, my lord. Promises? I planned to make none other than the same I gave to you today.' Fayth struggled to keep the whole truth of Edmund's plans inside. 'He promised to protect me and my lands if I took him as husband. Nothing more. But you interrupted that.'

Her husband could not find out who Edmund was, not now while he still faced death if their charade was uncovered. Shaken to her core by the events and accusations of this day and a fair amount of honest guilt, she dropped her hand and shook her head.

'Until I discover whether your words or your actions speak the truth, I will not consummate our vows, lady. Once I know…' His words drifted off and she shivered at the threat he implied.

The tense silence surrounded them until he stepped away from her. Now he stood in the doorway and she decided she could face no more this day—whether he be invader, husband, lord or whatever. Grabbing the edge of the door, she pushed it closed quickly, causing him to stumble out into the hall.

'Good night, then, my lord husband!' she said as she caught the latch and dropped the bar that had been left carelessly in the corner.

She did not delude herself into thinking he could not get back in if he chose to, for breaking the door would take only the kick of a strong man, and in addition to himself her new husband had an abundance of those available. His loud laughter from the other side of her door confused her. It was not the reaction she'd thought he would have to her act of defiance.

When no one entered or even tried to, Fayth walked around the room, blew out the candles and climbed into her bed. Tugging the headpiece from her hair and loosening it, she lay down in the middle of the bed and waited to find out if he would force his way back in.

A short time later, she could no longer fight the sleep that pulled at her mind and body. For once, Fayth pushed off the fears that coursed through her and gave in, sinking into the darkness without worrying about her fate.

Chapter Three

Fayth surprised Giles with every word she spoke and with every step she took. Most of the women he knew would have collapsed in fear during their assault on the keep and never had the courage to move forward with a bold move to marry the man who offered her the only chance at rescue.

Although she feared him, Giles knew the moment when anger replaced that fear for her eyes had flashed brightly and a rush of colour had filled her cheeks just before she had slammed the door in his face. Nearly on his face, if truth be told.

Most men in his situation would have broken through the door the instant it was shut in their faces, but he had held back then. Oh, one kick would break it down, but why cause more work for someone who would need to repair it or build a new one when he had the means to remove the door without damage? And using his fists was always his last choice of action, for any brute could pound down a lesser opponent. Giles wanted to be more than that in his dealings here as lord and husband, especially with such a woman as the lady who was now his wife.

Giles knew that his men watched him, not only the two guards standing nearest the door, but also those who had accompanied him to the wedding and back. Still, between her strength of character and her intelligence, he should not have been surprised. He stepped away then and turned to leave.

'Not quite the frail English flower you expected, then, eh?' Roger asked as they walked down the steps to the main hall.

'And even you could not have plucked that flower so quickly,' Brice said from behind him. 'You are good, *my lord,* but not that good.'

His men laughed at the insult as did he. *Plucking a flower* as beautiful as this one would not have been difficult at all and, considering the womanly curves and feminine enticements she offered, he could have managed a quick bedding in a very short time. If Giles gave himself leave to, he could have lost himself in the depth of her green eyes, but his fear about her true role in his enemy's plans haunted him too much.

He'd shared the truth of his concerns and his intention to avoid consummating their vows until he knew the truth of her condition only with Brice. Gaining a bride who'd lost her virtue was not the best situation, but he'd be damned before he accepted another man's child as his without knowing. The irony of his concerns was not lost on him.

'Ah, but we are Bretons,' Giles said, laughing. 'We are better than most and certainly faster than these Englishmen.' Smacking Brice hard on the shoulder, he nodded at him. 'And you, soon to be my Lord Thaxted, should be wary and watchful for you will have your own Saxon maid to deal with shortly.'

Brice remained silent, most likely thinking of the challenges he would face soon. Once things were in Giles's control here, Brice would be free to continue his journey north to gain the keep and the woman who would be his. Giles motioned for the others to precede him and issued new orders to the guards concerning his…wife.

Would there ever be a time when he did not stumble over such a thought? Born a bastard, the son of a Breton vicomte and a weaver, a common woman, he should never have aspired to such a position in life. Dreamed? Oh, yes, he had dreamed of it and prayed for such a thing, but a man such as he did not marry the daughter of a nobleman and gain a title as he had. By rights, he should be a servant in his father's household, but William's need for men to fight in his cause and Giles's own skills in the arts of warfare had brought him to this moment.

War, as his friend Simon would say, was a great leveller of men and an open avenue to advance past one's station in life. Giles smiled as he remembered their many conversations earlier this year on the occasion of Simon's marriage to Elise. It was the first step he'd taken on this road to his own destiny.

Still, having gained such a title and such a

wife did not wipe out the niggling doubt that moved through him each time he heard himself being called 'my lord'. It would take some time to answer that call easily or to think of the angry woman in the chamber as his wife…and even more time to accept that he was worthy of the honours given him by the king.

Once the guards understood their orders, he followed the others down the stairs to the hall where many still ate and drank of the wedding feast's bounty, such as it was. The fare at table was nothing but a beggar's meal if compared to some he'd seen in Brittany. Simon's went on for more than a day while his own half brother's feast went on for three days, with course after course of fowl and meat and fish and delicacies that yet made his mouth water even at the memory of them.

But neither his father, Simon nor the father of either of those brides had had to worry about their crops burning in the fields and barns. They did not have to spend a moment considering how many of their people would survive the coming war and the coming winter. With a beleaguered sigh after pushing those serious concerns aside for the moment, he climbed the few steps to the raised table and sat in the chair in the middle of it. Brice, Roger and several others of his men joined him there without much fanfare.

Giles tore a chunk of meat off a roast of… something and stuffed it in his mouth, chewing to soften up the tough piece before trying to swallow it. Even a mouthful of ale did not ease its path down to his stomach.

Then he noticed it.

Complete silence filled the hall. It seemed to start with the villagers present and then, when his men noticed it, they stilled as well. As one, they stared at him. Giles resisted the urge to see if he'd come naked to the table, so startled by their silent scrutiny. Leaning over to Brice, who sat at his side, he lowered his voice and spoke.

'What is the matter here?'

'You have attended weddings before, my friend. What do you think is the matter?' Brice whispered in their Breton tongue.

Giles surveyed the faces before him. They wore expressions of surprise and concern and even anger. The people had eaten their fill, drank of the ale and sat at their ease during the meal. Now, darkness called them to rest. Yet, their unhappiness and anger could be seen and felt and even heard as the silence gave way to hushed grumblings in that awkward tongue of theirs. He realised his error even as Brice spoke the words.

'They wonder how the groom can so quickly return to the wedding feast.' Brice leaned closer so that he could not be overheard. 'They know nothing of your concern about the lady's *condition*. They know only that you married her and have returned from your marriage bed within minutes of arriving there.'

Merde.

Giles drank down the cup of ale in his grasp and motioned for more. He'd not considered the ways in which his actions would be seen or even considered that any person, villein or free, in his hall might have a concern over them. As a bastard serving his lord, his actions mattered naught except when they interfered with his lord's desires or needs or commands. Now, it was his word that mattered. His actions were to be heeded and obeyed.

As he drank the ale again he shook his head at Brice. He'd arranged for them to say their marriage vows before her people to lessen the strain in the keep and village about her health. Rumours had flown round in the days after his arrival and her lack of presence had made them wonder whether he'd killed her or not. Only the word of her servants that she was alive had kept the worst of the distrust at bay.

Now this.

'This is a private matter between the lady and me.'

'Ah, my lord, you have it wrong there. Within hours, if indeed it takes that long, every person living within the walls or without will know what is between you and their lady. And that you have not consummated your vows.'

He gazed out over the tables before him, seeing the mutinous stares from those who would never dare to say a word. He could not, nay, he would not relent and bed Fayth before knowing the truth. His hand would not be forced in such a grievous matter.

'*Merde.*' This time he'd said the word aloud.

'Exactly, my lord.'

'I will not explain myself to them, Brice,' he said, clenching his teeth. Giles looked out over the hall and the people there. His illegitimate standing gave rise to his reluctance in this and he would not discuss it with anyone.

They knew nothing but what happened here, within these walls, within this small village. They knew not of his struggles to rise from his bitter beginnings, to gain fame and fortune in tourneys across his homeland, and to be worthy enough of this prize he'd received. They knew only of their lady and her father and their land and their crops and cattle.

Insulting her or the memory of her father while the rebels gathered throughout the con-quered lands and even just outside his lands was not the most intelligent thing he could do. Revealing his doubts about her state of purity or her part in plans to overthrow his lawful control of this holding might be appealing, but he knew that doing that would lead to ruin and uproar and possible rebellion.

For now, he must forbear any urges to strike out too quickly, he must assess his every move and, aye, he must take notice of the way his actions appeared to his people.

'You understand my actions, Brice. What would you suggest?'

Brice peered out over the people now gathered in the hall and then turned to him.

''Tis too late to change your actions in this, nor do I suggest you do, but try not to worsen it. They—' he nodded in the direction of those watching, ever silent in their disapproval '—understand more about your situation than I would guess you do. They know the lady, her late father, and the identities and location of those who sought to usurp your position here.'

Brice gifted him with a knowing look. Ah, so he, himself, had not been the only one to suspect that those now outlawed and their connections to Fayth and Taerford had not yet been revealed or severed completely. 'Go on.'

'You know what you must do, Giles. Think of Lord Gautier's counsel about how to act when others depend on your actions,' he said with a wave of his hand where no one else but Giles could see it. 'Treat the lady with respect. Take her to your bed as soon as possible, move on as you mean to go,' he began, lowering his voice. 'You have not been a…nobleman before. A baron now, a lord of this realm. This presents you with many new challenges never faced before, Giles, as it will to me shortly.'

Giles nodded in agreement. As the bastard son of a Breton nobleman, he had never been put in a position where others were under his control. Except for his men, the ones who had joined him in fighting with William the Conqueror, he had controlled no one but himself.

Until now. Now, he held property, he held power.

He had a noble-born lady as wife.

'And you? Will you follow your own wise counsel?'

Brice lifted his cup to Giles in a gesture of respect and nodded his head. 'I can see these things clearly for you. I only hope I can see them as clearly when I encounter them.'

Giles emptied his cup and placed the metal goblet on the table in front of him. All good counsel aside, there was one immediate problem looming before him—a place to sleep this night. He'd never intended to make her rejection such a public one. However, the sound of the bar securing the door had been unmistakable and the message clear to everyone who'd heard it.

'You allowed her to make her stand, now make yours,' Brice said as though reading his thoughts. 'If this breach remains a source for gossip, it makes you and this keep vulnerable to attack. To ensure that some may believe your outward actions, you might consider taking your hauberk off before seeking your lady.'

Giles laughed as he touched his chest. 'You did not see her anger when I left the room. I may not see the morn without it.'

He'd grown so accustomed to the protective layer, he'd not even removed it for his wedding. Now, considering the expressions in the lady's eyes as he'd forced her into marriage and then questioned her honour, the layers of interwoven iron rings might not be enough to keep him safe while he slept with her.

'My thanks for your wise counsel, friend.'

Standing, he moved away from the table and waved off the two guards who'd begun to shadow his movements. Giles called to the boy Martin to follow as he made his way through the door leading to the kitchen. The heat from the cooking fires, not yet banked for the night, blasted at him as he entered. Within moments, those working there noticed him and stopped and stared. This was one place in Taerford Keep where he had not established a presence, but he remedied that now.

After calling for a tub and pails of hot water, Giles was led by someone named Gytha to a small room just off the kitchen. He had planned only to remove as much of the dirt and dust as he could, but soon the sight of the steam rising from the water enticed him to make use of it. He laid his sword in its scabbard on the floor near the tub and then, with Martin's help, he unfastened and peeled off the layer of armour and mail he wore. He sent the boy, who was training to learn the ways of knights, away with instructions on its cleaning and oiling and closed the door for some measure of privacy.

He made quick work of removing his padded gambeson and shirt, adding those and his braies and boots to the pile of clothing on the floor. Giles stretched his arms towards the ceiling above and enjoyed the lack of the armour's weight on his body. It had been too long since he had last indulged in the pleasure of a real bath, using pails of water or even streams or rivers when available to him for the task. Now, a hot soak would ease his tension over his coming encounter with his new bride.

The next thing he knew the water was growing cold and a pile of clean clothes and drying linens lay on a bench next to the door. Looking around, he also found two buckets with steaming water within reach. He'd not given in to the exhaustion he'd felt for these last months, first battling in Brittany for his uncle's claim to the duchy and then supporting William's claim to England on behalf of his liege lord, Simon.

There'd been little time for the luxury of a hot bath and a leisurely bedding of an appealing woman. He still had months, if not years, of hard work ahead of him, but Giles could content himself in knowing that it was his lands, his keep and his woman. And, God willing, his children. But first, the matter of his wife begged his attention.

Filled with a fair amount of reluctance, he stood in the tub, finished washing the grime and sweat from his body and hair and climbed out. Drying himself off, he stretched again and then sought the clothes left for him. Tugging the shirt over his head, he recognised the quality of the garment and it took him but a moment to realise the origin of it—this was something left behind by the old lord when he had followed Harold to Hastings.

As were the braies and the tunic. The old earl was much broader in the shoulders and chest than Giles was, but these were the only clothes he could wear for now. Poor planning on his part, for the only garments he had lay locked in a chest in Lady Fayth's room.

He shook his head at his mistake and wrapped his belt around his waist, positioning his scabbard where he could reach it easily. Then he pulled on his boots and left the small chamber, using a set of back steps he found to get to the upper floor of the keep. Standing before the lady's chambers, he found the two guards as he'd left them.

Well, except for the metal hinges in their hands.

'A gift from Brice, my lord.'

Giles accepted Brice's gift and smiled. Brice could get in or out of any place, release any lock or find the weakness in any device. Without the hinges, the door could be manoeuvred out from under the bar. With the help of the guards, he did just that and it allowed him entrance with little noise. He waited while the door was placed against the frame and then walked over to the bed.

In spite of the control she exerted over her actions while awake, Lady Fayth slept with reckless abandonment. Reckless and enticing abandonment, even if still wearing her clothes.

She lay half on her side, half on her back, one arm was thrown to the side and the other lay across her forehead, blocking the top of her face from his view. Her legs, though covered by her smock and kirtle, relaxed apart, and the urge grew within him to slide his hand up and explore the area between her thighs. His body tightened as he walked closer and saw that her hair was loose.

She lay on top of most of it, the soft length pillowing around her head with a few loose tendrils softening the look of her face. In the darkened chamber, lit only by the flames in the hearth, it appeared much darker than in the light of day, when it caught the sunlight and blossomed with a multitude of hues of brown and lighter. His hands itched to touch it, to smell it, to rub it against his face and over their bodies as they made love.

Giles shook himself, trying to loosen the grasp of this desire now moving through him. He was no untried boy that his body should react so strongly to a woman. Truly, this woman had not tried to entice or entrance him; instead she'd stood up to him, refused his kindnesses and nearly repudiated his claim to her and these lands. Not the usual bed partner of one of the Breton Bastards, as he and his friends were called.

He walked to the side of the bed and leaned over, giving in to the urge to touch her. With a gentle stroke, he traced down the edge of her chin and her cheek. She murmured in her sleep and seemed to turn into his palm. Holding his breath, he sat carefully on the bed, easing across its surface, and cupped her face in his hand. When she threw her arm away from her head and it landed in his lap, nearly touching his cock, he knew he was lost.

And she slept on.

He almost regretted his pledge to her to withhold relations until she proved she was not carrying a child. Almost. Though it was a near thing when she turned slightly and her lush breasts pressed against the gown she wore. At least the extra fabric in the braies he wore afforded him some relief when his cock grew harder in anticipation.

Drawn to the innocence and the softened expression that sleep brought to her face, he watched as she breathed deeply and evenly. With her cheek still cupped in his hand, he let his thumb slide over her face and touch her lips. They were full and red; he imagined their feel against his. Trying to lessen the urge to take her and claim her, Giles glanced away from her mouth and at her face.

Eyes the color of the darkest forest leaves met his gaze.

Lady Fayth had awakened.

Chapter Four

First Fayth looked at Giles's eyes, then she seemed to remember where she was and who touched her in such a way. Then she moved, scrambling up and back away from him faster than he thought it possible to move. Within seconds, she knelt against the corner of the bed against the wall in a defensive position, meant to keep anyone at bay. All she needed to complete her formidable pose was a weapon in her hand.

'You sleep in your gown?' he asked in a soft voice, trying not to startle her.

'How did you get in here?' she asked back, ignoring his jibe completely.

'Once the hinges were gone—' he nodded at the doorway '—it was simply a matter of lifting the door and the bar out of the way.' Giles slid from the bed and faced her. 'Do not bar the door again.'

Her eyes widened in fear at his words or mayhap at the tone he used. When she brushed her hair out of her face, it flowed over her shoulders and down her back in long waves.

'Come,' he said, offering her his hand. 'Take your ease as you wish. Door or no door, you are safe here.'

Now, doubt warred with the fear in her eyes as her gaze moved from him to the doorway and back to the bed. He wondered if she was confused, as waking so suddenly from such a deep sleep could do. Backing a few steps away, he sat in a chair and waited for her to act.

'You said you would not,' she began, lowering her voice so that none outside the chamber could hear. 'You left with your men.'

'You pushed me from the chamber and barred the door behind me. I could not allow such an insult to go unanswered.'

The fear returned in her gaze and Giles discovered that he did not like it. Anger turned her eyes a flaming green, a shade that sparked with gold, but fear turned them flat and nearly colourless.

'Is it our joining you fear?' he asked. 'Or something else?'

Her cheeks flushed red and she looked away. Was she embarrassed by such frank words? She did not look ready to explain herself to him. Had she, in truth, given herself to Edmund or was this a maiden's blush?

'I told you it will not be until I know you carry no one else's babe, so come away from the wall and seek your rest.' He motioned with his hand.

'Why do you insult me so?' the lady asked as she slid over the bed and climbed off, straightening her gown and shaking it to cover her legs. Her hair tumbled over her shoulders in enticing waves. 'Do you think I hold my honour, and that of my father, with so little respect that I would succumb easily to the desires of the flesh?'

He was out of the chair in a second and standing so close to her that he saw her wobble and nearly lose her balance in trying not to touch him and yet looking up to meet his gaze. Giles watched her eyes widen and her breaths grow shallow as he stood, not moving, not touching, not breathing.

Heat grew between them, around them and within him until he burned from it. Not succumb to the desires of the flesh? From the fear now flashing in her eyes to the shaking of her limbs and the paleness of her skin, he suspected that she had not experienced the fires of passion that could erupt between a man and a woman. It did not mean that she'd not lost her virginity to someone else, but there was much he could show and teach her about desire.

For now, though, a simple lesson would suffice. More than that threatened his tenuous control and he must not allow that to happen...yet. Giles bent his head lower, forcing Fayth to tilt hers more. When he moved his lips so close to hers that he could feel her breath against his skin, he paused.

'Desires of the flesh, lady?' he asked, dipping even closer. 'But there is much to commend those desires.'

Fayth started to object, to explain the true meaning of her words, when his lips—already too close—touched hers. The heat given off by his body intensified with the touch of his mouth to hers and in her confusion, she forgot to close her lips. His tongue, hot and strong, surged into her mouth and sought the touch of hers. Not sure of what to do, she waited, fighting the unbelievable need to throw her arms around him and pull him closer.

Where that desire came from, she knew not, but an urge pulsed through her body then, as his tongue tasted hers, that brought all manner of wicked thoughts and feelings to mind. Fayth could tell he enjoyed the kiss, for he moved closer to her and pressed against her mouth, deepening the simple touch into something more possessive. Just as she was learning his rhythm, thrusting his tongue into her mouth, tasting her own and luring it into his mouth, he drew back and changed it into something different.

Now, he used his mouth on her lips, then, sliding lower, he kissed the edge of her jaw and her chin before moving to her neck. If she'd thought that his first kiss tempted her to more, this one or these many shocked her. With each touch of his mouth to her skin a shattering jolt moved from her skin to deeper inside until the very core of her ached. Moisture grew between her thighs and the unseemly urge to press against him strengthened until she thought she might...

When he reached out and lifted her hair off her neck and shoulders, she did reach for him. Feeling light-headed from holding her breath in excited anticipation, she clutched his tunic to steady herself. Still, he did not stop his attentions, now kissing nearer to her ear and higher on her neck. She thought he whispered something once, but, truly, she could not keep a thought in her head right then.

As he used one hand to loosen the ties of her smock and tug the edges of it open Fayth began to protest, but his mouth took hers in another breathless kiss until she gave up all attempts to make sense. Then he kissed and licked his way down to the opening he'd made, exposing the tops of her breasts to his sight and his touch.

Thankfully, she still clutched his tunic or she would have sunk to the floor as first his finger and then his lips and tongue traced a path there. The aching deep inside grew into a throbbing need she could not understand or ignore. She tried to draw in a deep breath, but it turned to a gasp as he suckled the skin at the top of one of her breasts. The urgent pulling and licking and even nipping at her flesh released a torrent of pleasure and created a longing she could not believe possible.

Fayth let go of his tunic and reached up to pull him closer and everything changed. It was as though her touch were abhorrent to him for he lifted his mouth from her skin, released her hair from his fisted grasp and stepped away from her. Stumbling from the weakness and excitement that pulsed through her, she fell to sit on the edge of her bed. The cool air of the chamber hit the wet, heated skin of her neck, shoulders and exposed breasts, and it shocked her back to her senses—the ones that should have warned her to put a stop to his indecent actions.

Giles watched her with an amused expression lighting his eyes and she suspected she'd fallen into a trap. And she had, for indeed her entire body ached for his touch, for his kisses and the intimate way he had used his tongue on her skin. Then she realised the purpose of his attentions and how he'd made her belie her claim about the desires of the flesh.

'Does your body not hunger for more, lady? Is there not an aching within to be touched in places you cannot speak of?' He stopped and looked as though he would come closer once more but he did not. 'If I slid my hand beneath your gown and smock and into that place between your legs, would I find you wet with desire?'

Fayth did gasp then, both at the vulgarity and truth of his words. She did not have to admit the truth; they both knew it.

'Just so,' he whispered as he turned away and strode to the table where their cups and wine still lay. 'And consider that it was only a kiss between us.'

With his back to her, he poured and drank two cups before stopping. She could see his body move as he took in and released several deep breaths of his own. Before he could face her, she gathered the edges of her smock together and tied the laces tightly, covering all that he had exposed and more. Pushing her hair out of her face and behind her shoulders, she pondered what to say.

Did she admit to her ignorance of the power of such feelings? The few kisses she'd exchanged with Edmund had been nothing like this, more an exchange of affection between old friends. She'd fancied herself in love with her father's cousin who'd visited two summers before, but it had been one-sided and Gareth never knew of her feelings so they had certainly not shared kisses such as these.

Only a kiss? Oh, no, he'd done more than simply kiss her tonight. He'd exposed a vulnerability she did not know existed as easily as he had exposed her breasts with a tug at her laces.

But the worst of it was that her body had reacted to the touch of a stranger, a man who had very possibly killed her father on the field of battle. With those few kisses and caresses, he'd made a fool of her and her valiant protests about her honour. Shame poured over her, dampening any remaining desire as she contemplated her weaknesses and the true power of errant desires of the flesh to lead one astray or to aid in compromising their honour.

Lord Giles stood before her, holding out a cup. How long he'd been there, she knew not, for she'd been lost in her thoughts. Fayth accepted the cup and drank deeply from it, hoping to ease the tightness in her throat with the cool wine. She could not meet his gaze and see the triumph there, so she walked past him to place the cup on the table.

Giles saw the shame in her downcast eyes and the way her shoulders slumped. He recognised it well enough, for his mother had carried it most days of her life. He cursed under his breath at his stupidity. Lady Fayth shuddered at his words.

'My lady, I but sought to show you the control that desire can exert, even on someone who thinks to resist its call.'

'And it has been a lesson well learned, my lord,' she answered. When she turned and faced him, he knew from the bleakness in her eyes and the paleness of her skin that they were not speaking of the same lesson.

Giles could not answer, for every word that

came to mind would not ease her embarrassment or would undermine the message he wanted to send to her. He nodded at the bed.

'Seek your rest, my lady. 'Tis been a long and trying day and much work faces us in the morn.'

She continued past him until she stood at the side of the bed. A glance over her shoulder at him and then at the chair and the floor and back to the bed spoke of her confusion over *his* place to sleep this night.

'Lady, climb in and seek sleep.' He walked to the bed and lifted the many layers of linen sheets, woollen blankets and even thick animal skins that covered the bed and offered warmth in the long, cold autumn nights. He did not ask her about removing her gown and tunic or even her stockings, for the fear within her was palpable to him.

She let out a deep breath and kicked off her shoes, sliding them under the edge of the bed. Lady Fayth lifted her gowns, climbed up and shifted over the bed, rearranging her many layers once she reached the other side. Giles dropped the coverings and let her find her place under them. When she seemed settled, he moved around the chambers, blowing out candles and banking the flames in the hearth, all preparations for the night.

'Will you sleep here?' she asked in a whisper.

'Aye, lady, I will seek my rest at your side.' He waited for her protests and when they did not come, he tried to explain. 'If I'd wanted to tup you like the barbarian you think me to be, it would have happened after the battle, when the heat of it yet burned in my veins and control of such passions are difficult. Or when I watched you lie senseless here those nights and could have had you without any protests. When I decide to have you, lady, you will not have a moment to spend worrying over my taking of you…it will happen.'

He blew out the last taper and began removing his tunic and shirt as he moved closer to the bed. He sat and tugged off his boots and then untied his breeches and let them drop. Leaving one layer of sheeting down, he lifted the rest and climbed within, allowing the lady her own clothing and the sheet as a barrier between them.

As he lay next to her in the dark, listening to

her low breathing and knowing she was backed up to the wall and as far as possible from him, he knew there were so many more barriers separating them and none were easily overcome. And, as his own body still pulsed with the desire for her that touching her and kissing her and stroking her caused, he tried remembering why he thought it such a good thing to teach her about passion. The blood that rushed through his veins and made his cock stand confirmed that he could be caught in the same trap he set.

So much for lessons to learn.

Fayth knew she'd not slept a wink all night, not with the stranger sleeping naked so close to her. Yet, when she found him gone as the sunlight finally pierced through the veil of night and she had no recollection of his leaving, she knew that sleep must have claimed her unaware at some moment earlier.

Her back ached from being pressed against the hard surface of the wall all night, trying to keep her distance from the very large, very warm body in her bed. If he was troubled by what had occurred between them, his manner of falling immediately into the embrace of sleep and breathing deeply through the long night spoke not of it.

Rubbing her eyes, she allowed a yawn to escape before dragging her body across the bed to its edge. Her *cyrtel* and *syrce* twisted around her legs and waist and Fayth tugged it down in place just as the door of the chamber opened, or was moved away from the frame. Fearing another encounter with her new husband, she was comforted when her maid entered instead. Within minutes, a tub and buckets of steaming water were brought into the room and set up in front of a fire in the hearth.

In Emma's care, her own worries fell away as her maid issued stern commands about placing the door back on its hinges and huffed about the chamber protecting Fayth's privacy during her bath. Once satisfied that the door, jammed against the frame, would be an able barrier to anyone entering, she turned and faced Fayth. With a frown and grimace at finding her in her gown and barely a pause to acknowledge it, Emma efficiently lifted the outer tunic off, un-laced the long sleeves and loosened the *cyrtel* and finally the linen shift. Then she lifted all the remaining layers over Fayth's head. Her maid's unstifled gasp made her turn sharply at the object of Emma's concern.

There on her breast was a mark, a bruise of a sort marring her skin. She laid her fingers there, but there was no pain as she would have expected, but her skin felt heated.

'Did he hurt you?' Emma whispered, nodding at the mark as she busied herself shaking out Fayth's clothing. 'Did he, my lady?'

First waves of embarrassment filled her. Then the realization that Emma thought Lord Giles had done this. The worst was when the truth struck her and Fayth knew that the passionate kiss Giles had placed there, the one when he had used his lips and tongue and even his teeth, had left such a mark. She felt the heat in her cheeks and her breasts even ached as she remembered the pleasure of it and even as she tried to find words to say to Emma.

'He...I...' she stuttered, not knowing whether to explain or not.

'Hush, now, lady,' Emma said. The old woman

guided her to the waiting tub and helped her step inside. 'The hot water will soothe you.'

Fayth decided not to protest or to explain something so personal as this. Sinking into the bath, she could not meet Emma's gaze. Inhaling the pleasant scent of the herbs and oil added to the water, Fayth tried to put her fears out of her mind for the moment and it would have worked if not for Emma's whispered words.

'How could he do something like this?' The maid continued her work around the tub and continued her diatribe against their new lord as well, still in hushed tones. 'I thought he had more sense than to mistreat an innocent.'

'He does not believe me an innocent,' she blurted out.

'Not innocent, my lady? I would swear on my mother's grave, may she rest in peace, that you are as pure as the day you were born.' Emma, her nurse, then maid and now friend, too, would be one who knew it.

'And this new lord would believe you not, Emma. He accused me of giving myself to Edmund and carrying his child.'

Emma dropped the soapy washing cloth into

the water and gasped. Stumbling back from the tub, she shook her head. Fayth could tell when shock gave way to anger, for Emma's round face grew red and beads of sweat, not related to the task at hand, began to roll down her forehead and cheeks. Leaning back closer, she whispered once more to her, glancing first behind her as though to see if anyone had entered.

'But surely, my lady, he discovered the truth? When he bedded you?' Emma took Fayth's hand from where it lay on the edge of the tub and stroked it gently. 'Fear not, lady. I always keep your confidences.'

Fayth's resolve not to speak of such matters, even though Emma had held her counsel in the two years since Fayth's mother's death, dissolved then in the face of Emma's kind-hearted concern and in knowing that Emma would carry her secrets, if she knew them, to the grave.

'He did not bed me. He said that until he knows I am not carrying a child, he will not. And he did not believe me when I told him I have not given myself to anyone.'

Spilling out the words brought a deep sense of sadness to her. As daughter and heiress to her father, her word had always been accepted, her honour never questioned. Sliding forward and wrapping her arms around her knees, she laid her face there and thought on it as Emma attended to her back and began washing her hair.

'Hush now, lady. All will be well. At least he did not take you roughly or against your will,' she offered as she lathered up the length of Fayth's hair. But instead of soothing her troubled thoughts, her words added to them.

'Emma, how can it be other than against my will? This man attacks my people, takes my lands and forces me to marriage. I do not want this and I suspect he does not want me either.' Emma's hands stilled and Fayth could swear the woman stifled a laugh.

'I know he covets what I bring to him, Emma. I am no fool in that regard. But I want him no more than he wants me.' Tears threatened then and her throat tightened as she thought on her reaction to his touch and to his kiss. 'I cannot want him,' she whispered.

Emma did not press her for more and Fayth was glad of it. The fact that her body came to life under his touch shamed her and she did not wish to repeat such a weakness again. They accomplished the rest of her bath in silence and Fayth stood so that Emma could rinse her of the soap. Allowing the water to pour down over her, Fayth closed her eyes.

The sound of his loud, angry voice preceded that of the door crashing against the wall by only moments.

'I told you not to bar this door,' he yelled, but then his voice dropped lower, much lower when he looked at her, 'to me.'

Chapter Five

The sight of Lord Giles standing there, filled with anger, fist still raised and glaring at her gave Fayth pause. She did not dare move, for it was only his tall body that blocked those behind him. Fayth heard Emma's indrawn breath behind her and, as she watched, the warrior's gaze moved over her nakedness.

Her skin tingled wherever his eyes looked— first her face and neck and then her breasts as she saw the glimmer of recognition as he noticed the mark there. Then his gaze slid down until he stared at her legs and the area between them. The tips of her breasts tightened under his bold, sexual stare and shock finally gave way to action. She covered herself as she could with her arms and hand while reaching for a drying cloth, one which Emma could not seem to find.

Fayth turned her back to him, chancing even more of his anger, to grab the large cloth from Emma's hand and to wrap it around herself. For some reason, her maid did not move to aid her and it took some moments for Fayth to accomplish. It was then that she heard Emma's whispered words.

'I do not think you need to worry about him wanting you, lady.'

Fayth turned and faced her husband, whose expression had changed from anger to lust in those few moments. Now, his eyes burned hers with a heated stare. His hands fisted and released several times before he let them hang at his sides. Lord Giles wore his mail hauberk once more with his sword at his side, apparently ready for battle.

Realising she still stood in the tub, Fayth leaned down to hold the edge while stepping out. Before she could manage, he warned off his men and strode across the chamber in a few steps. Lifting her from the water and holding her high against his chest, he carried her over to the side of the bed and placed her on her feet. As she thought to thank him, Fayth was horrified to realise that she'd wrapped her arms around his neck and was still holding him so.

Once she released her grasp, he stepped back but his eyes stared lower and she noticed that the drying cloth had parted over her chest, revealing her breasts to anyone standing close or who stood as tall as he. Fayth tucked the edges tighter and thanked him.

'I did not bar the door, my lord.'

He was bold, she would admit to that, for he smiled wickedly in that moment, glancing at her now-covered breasts and then at her mouth.

'I see that, my lady.' He nodded to her then and threw a glance at Emma. 'I did not mean to invade your privacy either. Would you join me for the noon meal in the hall?'

He'd been speaking in her tongue and his deep voice made it sound so enticing, even when he stumbled over some of the words. Though most nobles in the land spoke varying forms of French, few nobles from the continent, let alone those of lesser standing, knew the English of her country. Yet, he tried to use it.

'Yes, I will join you.'

He offered a quick bow and nearly ran from

the chamber, calling out something to his men in his dialect. Fayth listened as his steps faded in distance and sound and then, when the door was jammed once more into place, she sat down on the bed in a heap.

What had she been thinking to stand so before him and not cover herself immediately? The terrible lapse could only have lasted a few seconds, but why had Emma allowed it at all?

The deeper, more telling question she asked herself in those few moments was why did he affect her so? Oh, she knew that just by his position as new lord and husband he affected her, but somehow it was more than that. His voice and his touch wrought such confusion and excitement within her when fear and loathing should be her reaction. It seemed that her wits and judgement were crumbling around her much as her world and life had.

In only two short months, her life had been twisted and turned until she no longer recognised it or herself. From beloved daughter to orphaned war-prize. From betrothed maiden to rejected wife. From loyal Englishwoman to the wife of a foreign enemy. It was no surprise then that she knew not how to act or what to think or feel!

Now she was all that stood between the conquerors and her family and people and it was time to remember that she was Fayth, daughter of Bertram, thane and earl of Taerford, and carried a proud legacy in her blood from her Saxon and Dane ancestors. Dressing quickly with Emma's help, she decided it was time to take the first steps at reclaiming herself and her people.

In spite of his hard labour, chopping the felled trees into smaller chunks and hauling them to the storage area near the stables, the desire for Fayth that raged through Giles's veins had not lessened. And presently, even after three hours had passed and he stood naked to the waist so that the cool air could ease the heat within him, it still sent a pulse through his body and kept his cock hard and ready.

He'd worked for the whole first hour or so in full chainmail before he allowed himself to slow down and remove it. Luckily, the bulk and weight of the hauberk covered most of the evidence of his reaction to seeing his wife in such a state. Then working himself to exhaustion was the only way he could keep himself from running back inside the keep, peeling off whatever the lady was wearing at the moment, and claiming every inch of the body he'd seen.

The sight of the creamy skin, pert, rose-tipped breasts and the shapely curves of her body had nearly undone him and the memories of her haunted him even now. The fading bruises on her neck had given him pause, but then he noticed the newer mark he'd left on the top of her breast last night. His mouth watered at the memory of her skin under it and once more his body readied itself to take her.

Damn! He'd gone to ask for her help and when faced with her stunning beauty and nakedness he'd stood, awestruck and unable to say a word. Then with a hurried request, he'd run and tried to work off his arousal so he could deal with her in a more controlled manner.

With a lifted arm, he wiped the sweat from his brow and surveyed the yard to see how work progressed. The wall and main outlying buildings were now in good stead and could withstand an attack. The keep was designed strangely, unlike any keep or castle he'd yet seen, for its innermost wall was of stone with the rest being wooden. So some rooms, like the kitchen and his chamber and the smaller one as well, could have stone hearths, while braziers were used for heat in the chambers farther away from the central wall.

He still had no idea of how many villagers had stayed behind or had followed Edmund and his men into the forests and he must find that out. They needed an accounting of all of that and their other supplies as well and it need be done quickly so that they could gather everything together and guard it from attack or pilfering, for November was full upon them and the winter winds and cold would howl soon. Stay alive, strengthen the walls, fight off attacks and hold these lands until spring—those were his only goals and every action he planned and carried out were aimed at those.

Yet, here he stood with lust rushing through his veins, thinking about inconsequential things like passion when critical things remained undone. He wanted the fair Fayth of Taerford and he would have her, but it would not be until he knew the truth and standing here yearning for her would do no good in the face of his every other needed task.

There was a moment last night when he'd questioned his chosen path in dealing with her, a moment when he'd recognised the deep hurt in her eyes when he'd doubted her word and wanted to believe her. Too much depended on him dealing with this whole situation well to simply cave in to the desire and the lust that coursed through his blood even now.

Too much.

Just then, a gap-toothed boy of about eight years ran up with a bucket of water and held out the dipper to him. After drinking the first two then pouring the rest over his head and his chest, Giles realised that his wasteful action would make the boy need to refill the bucket again for those waiting for a drink. He laughed then, more at himself than the boy, for no lords either Breton or English would have given a moment's consideration of it.

The look on the boy's face reminded him of himself at that age, for the job of water boy had been his at that time. He had run through his father's yards and brought water to all the men training there. And it was exhausting work, hauling the bucket to and fro the well, and re-filling it from the depths and carrying it again. No one but he would understand the difficulty of the task, certainly not most lords who never faced that kind of labour.

Giles understood.

Giles took the bucket back from him and motioned for the boy to follow. He knew he'd said the right word in their English tongue, *come,* yet the boy remained rooted in place. He repeated it and waved the boy towards the well and finally the boy followed, though he did not keep up with Giles's longer strides.

By the time he'd reached the well near the smithy's hut, a man stood by the boy, head and eyes lowered but still watching him. Then he noticed that many watched from their places in the bailey. All in silence, yet nothing moved that they did not see. Turning back to the well, he spoke to the man.

'Your name?' he asked as he checked the

knot on the rope holding the dipping bucket. He tossed the pail over the edge of the well.

'I am Hallam, my lord,' the man said, bobbing his head even lower. Glancing between the two as the bucket splashed below into the water, he thought that they might be father and son.

'Is this one your son, then?' Giles nodded at the boy as he walked to the other side of the well.

'Aye, my lord. His name is Durwyn.' Hallam stepped closer to his son and then asked, 'Has he done something to displease you?'

Giles saw the nervousness now in both their behaviour and in those watching the scene from where they stood. 'Durwyn did nothing wrong, Hallam. I am but filling the bucket from the well.'

Leaning over, he checked to see that the bucket sank deep enough to fill and then grabbed hold of the handle of the windlass and cranked until the bucket appeared over the stone edges. Giles lifted the overflowing pail, turned to fill Durwyn's bucket and met their gaping expressions. Finishing the task before stopping, he held the bucket out to the boy.

'For all that I used, Durwyn,' he said, smiling.

Hallam pushed the boy forward and Durwyn took the bucket and ran off, trying not to spill more of it than he kept.

'My thanks to you, my lord, for helping the boy,' Hallam said, bowing again and backing away. It was not until Hallam returned to his own task that Giles realised the misstep he'd taken.

Giles was lord here. Not water boy or servant living on the pleasure of their lord any longer. He was lord now...here. It was difficult to shake off memories of his past though.

Too many years working in menial, back-breaking tasks. Too many reminders that he was not worthy of more. Too much time spent watching those designated worthy, simply for being given a name, gain much for naught else but that name.

Only Simon's father, who'd gathered three bastard boys from their noble fathers, had seen that ability and skill could mean something and had saved him and Brice and Soren from the life that befitted bastard sons. Training them even as he trained his noble-born son, Simon's father had branded them with his own ideals of fairness, hard work and confidence in their abilities.

Now, though, keeping those ideals in mind while taking on this new position was a testing of his abilities and his own honour. To know where the line was that separated the classes and when to approach it, when to ignore it and when to respect it were his daily challenges. Watching the father and son walk away, Giles knew it would be a constant battle for him.

Working with the axe and rebuilding required skill and strength, something expected of a warrior, so that would not diminish his standing. But helping a boy fetch water was not— it was servants' work. Looking around at the still-present signs of battle and knowing that hardship faced them even now, Giles realised it was a ridiculous distinction and shook off any regrets at working alongside his men to ready the keep for the coming winter.

Pomp and ceremony, aspects of being a nobleman, would have to wait until their survival was assured. Turning around, he strode off toward the yard, examining his next plan in his mind.

This one involved Fayth and he wondered how it would play out once she heard it.

Fayth made her way throughout the keep, checking each of her people, enquiring of their conditions and seeking news of others, others who'd been killed or left with Edmund. Grief filled her as she learned the names of her father's soldiers killed during the attack and those who'd died of their wounds. Worse, many villagers innocent of anything but trying to survive had been injured or watched their cottages and fields burned by the attacking forces.

And her heart hurt to learn of the many men who'd followed Edmund into exile. She'd known all of them almost from birth and their experience and skills would be sorely missed in a time of peace and prosperity, even more so during these troubled times.

The only thing that gave her some hope was that the new lord seemed to be treating her people fairly. He'd spoken directly to the cook about the man who'd attacked his daughter and given his word that Ardith would be safe from further harassment. He'd ordered villagers to the keep for their protection and made certain that they had food and shelter. He'd not imprisoned any free man who pledged fealty to him.

None of it matched the fearsome rumours about the invading forces that were pillaging and raping their way across England, spreading from the main battle in the south and moving north to control all of it. The fighting and killing was not complete and many more would die before the struggle for control of the throne was won.

Fayth sighed. So many dead and so much lost to the hunger of men for power and lands. And those not dead already faced the dangers of starvation and sickness and more during the approaching winter. Somehow she must find a way to work with the new lord in order to help her people survive. She turned and took the cloak from Emma's hands and tossed it around her shoulders as they left the kitchens and entered the yards.

The winds buffeted her, but Fayth stood for a moment outside the door and let them. She'd been within the keep for days and days and it weighed on her more than she'd realised until now. Emma reached out to tuck the edges of her linen veil, a sign of her new position as a married woman, under the cloak to keep the winds from tearing it free.

The last time she'd walked in the yard, she'd followed the Breton to the chapel and her marriage vows. This time she turned her face up to the sun's lights and enjoyed the smell of the autumn changes. Fayth knew that the number of sunny days would decrease now, until winter's cold and darker days crept over and controlled the lands and sky, so she used this fair-weather day to continue to seek out her people and determine their needs.

An hour passed and then another and Fayth lost herself in feeling needed once more. Though she'd not asked her husband's permission to do so, she took note of the needs amongst the people and what supplies they'd used and what were still available to them. Serving these last two years as her father's chatelaine had forced her to look objectively at the situation around her and to consider the coming winter's demands. As she approached the smith's newly rebuilt work cottage she caught sight of the

Breton knight leading Durwyn towards the well. Uncertain of his purpose, she shushed Emma and waved her away while she kept to the shadows thrown by the wall and keep while following them.

Fayth stood too far away to hear his words, but Durwyn's father spoke to the lord and from the glances they threw towards the boy she knew he was the centre of their discussion. The knight did not seem to threaten the boy, but she noticed that everyone carrying out their duties in the yard now watched the exchange. Soon, the boy went off carrying a freshly drawn bucket of water and the lord went back to his tasks.

Wearing next to nothing.

As he passed close by she leaned against the wall so she could not be easily seen by him. He'd been working at some labour that had left him sweating and he'd stripped off his tunic and shirt and worked only in his braies, which lay dampened against his skin. The cool air did not seem to chill him. His muscles moved as he did and she watched his powerful legs stride across the yard to where his men worked cutting up trees they'd felled around the outer edges of the wall.

This was the first time she'd seen him in daylight without clothing covering his form and she discovered an unseemly curiosity about the man who'd shared her bed. He called out something in his native tongue to one of his men, something about his days at his father's estate, and they laughed before he picked up the large axe and began to swing it around and down, chopping large pieces of trees into smaller logs that would be burned or chopped into planks for other needs.

Giles Fitzhenry, now Baron of Taerford, was as much a mystery now as when she'd received the missive informing her that he was on his way to take her lands...and her. Fayth stepped from the shadows and walked back to where Emma stood speaking with a few of the older women from the village. She listened as they spoke and shared confidences, but she could not take her gaze off the man who was now her husband.

His shoulders were broad and his arms and legs well muscled. Not as bulky as her father was, he stood taller than most of his men, save one. The one he called Brice. Both men were stripped to their braies and matched each other, stroke for stroke, in some unnamed competition that had the men beginning to cheer for one or the other.

When he turned to answer someone's call, she was gifted with the sight of his equally muscular chest, liberally sprinkled with hair that tapered under the edge of his loosely tied breeches. What would that feel like to touch? His chest and stomach rippled as he lifted and swung the axe, over and over, and in time with his friend. Suddenly, Fayth found it difficult to breathe and a wave of heat passed through her. Peeling off the cloak, she loosened the veil around her neck and tried to take a breath.

'Here now, my lady,' Emma said, taking the cloak from her and draping it over her own arm. 'You look a bit flushed.' Her maid reached out and touched Fayth's face and cheek. 'Praise God, no fever, you are just overheated…'

She didn't finish her words, and Fayth realised that the three women were following the direction of her gaze and seeing what, or rather whom, she watched. With a shared glance of their own from one to the other that bespoke of some common knowledge, they smiled at her and nodded.

'Worry not, my lady. It will wear off,' Alfrida, the smith's wife, said with a knowing smile.

'And mayhap not,' Riletta, the tanner's wife, said with her own enigmatic smile.

The three looked at her and then burst out laughing. So loud were they that the very man she had been watching stopped and turned towards her. Her face burned now and she could only hope he could not see it from across the distance. Fayth wanted to pull her veil farther forward to cover as much as possible, but stopped herself.

It was not as though she'd never heard the bantering amongst the women before, about their husbands and their bedplay. In the past, she'd disregarded it for her own marriage had been far off and a young maiden had no reason to listen to such gossip. Then, when her father had announced her possible betrothal to a distant cousin from Scotland, such talk had become interesting and she had listened more than a girl in her virginal state should have.

Now, faced with a husband whose physical needs were sometimes clear and sometimes a mystery to her, the intimations were daunting yet enticing. Her mouth went dry when she thought of him holding her against his chest, the one so clearly displayed to her now. But before she could embarrass herself with a mis-spoke word or gesture, a shrill whistle pierced the air. Turning to find its source, instead she saw the Breton warriors scrambling along the wall.

All of the knights and men-at-arms in the yard began arming themselves and Fayth froze, not knowing what to do or where to go. A few moments later, one of the men, Roger she thought his name was, stepped to her side and took her by the arm.

'Come, my lady. My lord would have me see you and the women to safety inside the keep.'

The man did not pause as he spoke, only held on to her and guided the others quickly inside. Her last glance back at her husband found him tugging his shirt back into place as his squire held his gambeson, mail shirt and weapons at the ready.

'What is happening?' she asked as she walked briskly into the main hall. Looking around, she found all of the women and children gathered there.

'Riders approach and Lord Giles is not certain of their identities. You will be safe here,' he said as he nodded at several other warriors there.

With some signal she did not see, the soldiers placed the women and children in a group near the stone wall and positioned themselves between them and the rest of the hall. Tables were turned on their edges and pulled together into a barrier wall. A defensive placement so that they stood between any intruders and the weakest ones in the keep. The windows, high up on the walls, were shuttered, keeping both the sun's light and any arrows aimed there out.

So much for a lovely autumn day.

Chapter Six

Fayth lifted one of the small children into her arms, trying to calm her while the girl's mother did the same with her other children. Even if they could not understand what transpired, the wee ones felt the danger and began to whimper or cry as the room grew dark. Everything that happened brought back memories of the attack on the keep by Giles's men just weeks before. Her heart pounded in her chest and she began to pace a few steps back and forth, trying to ease the little girl's distress as much as her own.

Could it be Edmund coming to rescue her? Coming to oust the Breton devils from her lands and keep? Had other loyal Saxons banded together to push Duke William from England? Would there be more bloodshed? And how many would die this time? Questions raced through her thoughts and she could only pray that, whatever happened, no one else would die.

At the sound of loud yelling outside, between the keep and the wall, Roger ordered them all to the floor behind the tables and Fayth sat there, whispering soothing words that she did not feel or believe to the girl in her arms. Readying his men, Roger gave them some signal and some hurried orders that she could not understand. The seconds turned into minutes and still there was no word or movement inside or out.

Realising that there were no sounds of battle or attack, Fayth permitted herself to hope this would end with no lives lost. The tension grew inside the keep until the sounds of approaching soldiers increased. Everyone peeked over the barricade and watched the doors that led to the yard, waiting and watching for the attack to come.

Then, a shrill whistle could be heard outside and Roger and his men relaxed their stance. Staying in position, they watched until the doors opened and Giles entered, leading a small group of his men. With a nod, Roger helped Fayth to her feet but bade her to wait at his side for Giles's arrival.

It took a few more minutes, for Giles stopped to speak to some of the soldiers and give additional orders or instructions and to ask questions, but all was accomplished in a voice and tone too low for her to hear. His last stop before reaching the enclosure behind which she stood was Roger.

Their exchange continued for several more minutes, sparing her several glances which she could not interpret. Tempted to push the table aside and leave on her own, she understood that she could gain information if she listened to them speak. Information about Edmund perhaps or about other Normans in the area. Instead, their words were low and hushed and she gained no insight into the riders' identities or Edmund's whereabouts.

Finally, as those guarding her and the others began moving the tables aside, the warrior reached the front of the room. Nodding to Roger and holding out a hand to her, he led her away from the rest.

'You follow orders well, my lady,' he said as

they stopped near the door to the yard. His nod in some way acknowledged or saluted her actions.

'I did not think I had a choice but to do so,' she answered. 'Who were they?' She lifted her hand from his armoured one. The feel of the metal reminded her once more of their first meeting in the chapel and she shivered at the memory of it.

'The unfortunate results of war,' he said. He turned and issued more orders before giving her his attention once again. She noticed that all of his men obeyed without question or pause, as though they'd fought and worked together for a long time. 'Not all of the Duke's men are willing to wait for their just rewards and ride out from London seeking easy targets to claim as their own.'

'Does it surprise you that there is no honour amongst thieves?'

The words slipped out before she thought on them and his reaction was swift. Taking her by the arm, he led her to the stairs and nodded at them.

'Seek your chambers and remain there until

I call for you,' he said loudly. He gestured up the steps and called out to Roger. 'See the lady to her chambers and report back to me.'

'My lord,' she began.

Fayth should know better than to provoke him, especially following so close to this dangerous situation, but sitting in the darkened hall, waiting for another attack on her keep and her people, had worn on her temperament. Now words failed her and, even more, the urge to apologise soured her mouth before she could speak such words. Still, he controlled everything and everyone here, so an attempt at humility was needed or she would find herself a prisoner in her chambers.

He shook his head at her and turned away, but she reached out and touched his arm. 'I fear this terrifying situation has overwhelmed me, my lord. Forgive my rash words spoken without thought.'

She looked neither terrified nor overwhelmed, but Giles hesitated to call her a liar even though she'd called him a thief. Instead he saw a glimmer of pride and something else, too, something less definite and more unidentifiable. Almost a challenge to call her bluff in this.

But there was much to do before dark and he could waste time standing here trying to discern her thoughts and her motives. If nothing else, this unexpected approach by strangers made clear the holes in his defensive plans for the keep, exposing gaps in both numbers and placement of men, weapons and strategies. There was much work to do to secure this place and in this situation the only thing that had saved them was that the riders were allies and not enemies.

'Very well, lady. See to the righting of the hall and see that the women go back to their assigned chores.'

She nodded, nearly bowing her head to him, and turned to the task he'd given her. He did not miss the smile that threatened there on her lovely mouth. It was as he suspected—there was no humility in her words or her actions. The lady was simply protecting her own intentions.

Part of him wished to strike out at her for her boldness, but he understood how much he needed the lady and her support. Being open enemies would turn the keep and the people into a personal battleground, one that would not stand against attacks from the outside. Oh, he could punish her, but after the small incident of giving assistance to the water boy and having every person in the yard stand witness Giles knew any goodwill gained would be lost if he took action against their lady for what seemed a trifling matter.

Instead, he left her to her task and made his way out into the yard. His commanders—Roger, Lucien and Matthieu, all Bretons he'd fought with for years—knew what he expected and so he found his horse saddled and six men, armed, at the ready. Giles mounted, accepted his shield from Martin and led the men out of the gates, which were closed behind them.

It would take him hours to ride the lands, checking for signs of either the gangs of rebels that had been formed amongst those opposed to or displaced by the arrival of Normans or, now, the gathering outlaw companies of Duke William's men who were taking what they wanted in ever-widening circles extending out from London.

Giles and his men arrived back at Taerford Keep just as the darkness of night lay completely across the lands. Luckily, a nearly full moon's light gave them some aid in making their way across the unknown hills and valleys of the lands he now controlled. At his signal, a whistled one practised many times, Roger ordered the gates open for them from his place in the guard tower. The small troop rode through and the gates were secured behind him.

Some men who were assigned to the stables met them and took the horses and Martin followed at his heels, knowing his duty to the knight he served. Giles sent the other men off to take their ease and have a good meal to replace the one they'd missed during their search. His own stomach growled loudly for, as they passed by the corridor that led to the kitchen, he could smell the aromas of something roasted and something baked.

When he was seated at table, weapons handed off to Martin for cleaning and mail removed, a large, steaming bowl of stew with a small round of cheese and some bread was placed before them, and he reported their discoveries to Brice, Roger and the rest.

A small band was taking refuge in the woods to the west of the keep. Giles had found the remnants of a camp along with fires and refuse, though they could not tell how many stayed there or who they were. He did not wish it disturbed until they could discover who was using it and for what purposes.

The meal finished and they still talked and planned, huddling around the table, even as the peasants from the village and the serfs began to settle into the hall for the night. With dangers encroaching from many directions, Giles knew he needed to be prepared and knew it meant the difference between survival and destruction. Roger's report that Lady Fayth had been helpful in organising those now living within the walls gave him hope that she would agree to continue to help him.

When one of the servants came over with news that a bath was prepared for him, he stood and excused the men to their rest for the night. After checking about the guards on duty, he washed quickly and climbed the steps to his, *their,* chambers. Smiling as he noticed that the door had been repaired and placed back on its hinges, he lifted the latch and pushed quietly against it.

Giles had seen many sides to the woman who was now his wife, but the sight that greeted him was a new one. He half expected to find her fully clothed in bed, with her back pressed against the wall. Instead, she sat in the one tall-backed chair in the room, wrapped in a blanket and sound asleep. Unlike earlier today in the yard, her hair lay loose around her shoulders, giving her face a much younger appearance.

Lady Fayth sighed then and shifted in the chair and one corner of the blanket fell loose. She mumbled then, some words that slurred together into an unintelligible sentence or phrase in her language. She settled again, once more into sleep's embrace, and he continued to observe her for a few more minutes before preparing for sleep himself.

Giles moved about the chamber, tugging the layers of furs and blankets down on the bed, tossing his garments on a trunk, and then decided it would be best to have the necessary conversation here, in private, than in view of her people or his. If she agreed to his request, fine, but if not, it did not bode well for their future. Crouching down in front of her, he touched her cheek and spoke her name softly. When he repeated it for the third time, her eyes began to flutter open.

He knew the moment she recognised him and the place where they were, for a look of fear entered her gaze. He realised that fear always entered her eyes at each of their encounters, something he was growing to dislike. She tried to back away. Considering that she sat in such a chair as she did, it was not possible, and it took a few moments for her to wake up fully.

'Lady,' he said softly. 'I did not think you meant to sleep the night in that chair.' He tapped on the arm of it and nodded to it. 'It does not offer much comfort.' He stood up then and took a step back and away. 'Surely, the bed is a better place? No?'

Fayth lifted her hand and rubbed her eyes to clear the sleepiness from them. She'd waited for hours here, first pacing to stay awake and then sitting here, praying for the souls of those killed on her behalf and for the innocents caught in the attacks. When she could no longer focus on the words, she'd closed her eyes for but a moment. From the way the candles burned low, she'd slept much longer than a moment. She noticed then his gaze fell to the prayer beads that helped her keep track of her prayers.

'Has good Father Henry watched over your souls for a long time?' he asked.

'Many years,' she said, gathering the beads and placing them on the table.

'Did he clerk for your father as well or did another see to those duties?'

Fayth thought that might be the first time he'd asked about her father directly and wondered at it. She tried to keep the pain in her heart under control as she answered him, but it hurt badly to think of her father as gone from her.

'Father Henry has served God here by taking care of our souls and served my father as clerk, my lord. I have been told that they grew up together and both were happy when Father Henry was sent by the bishop.'

Tears burned her eyes as she thought on the two of them over the many years. Swallowing against the tightness in her throat, Fayth cleared it and asked, 'Why do you ask, my lord? Have you need of a new priest or clerk?'

He did not answer her immediately; instead he looked away and began to pace, much as she did when troubled or deep in thought. Then he stopped a few paces from her and nodded. 'A clerk, I think, to take up those duties as well as a miller, a chandler, a reeve, a woodward, a brewer and a harpist, as near as I can tell. And, a few more villeins to take on some other of the duties in my Taerford demesne.'

'A harpist? We did not have a harpist here… before your arrival.'

He smiled then, one that curved his mouth most attractively and caused her blood to rush. 'Ah. But I have always found the music of the harp to be soothing and pleasant. We Bretons are amongst the best at playing it.'

He was delaying his true purpose, she could feel it, so she decided to ask him directly. 'What is your purpose here, my lord? What is it you wish to know?'

Giles stood straighter now and crossed his arms over his chest. 'I wish to know,' he began and then shook his head. 'I need to know how many and which of your people fled with Edmund.'

'I will not endanger those who made good their escape, my lord,' she said, pushing off the blankets she'd wrapped around herself and standing. 'You cannot expect me to be a traitor to them?'

He shook his head and waved her off. '*Non.* No. I expect no such thing from you, lady. But, if we are to protect those still here and survive further attacks and the coming winter, I need your help to take an accounting of whom and what remains now.'

Although she'd been thinking on the very same subject all day, his bringing it up to her shocked her. 'My help?'

'Aye. First I need to know which man I can trust as steward.'

Startled, she turned to face him. 'You would trust one of my people to serve as your steward?'

'Within reason.' He tilted his head and watched her closely as he answered. 'He will work closely with one of my men until I know if he is trustworthy or not. There is much work to do to prepare for winter and I need an able-bodied, intelligent man to carry out those measures.'

The proposal came to her mind in that instant and she blurted out the words before thinking it through. 'Must it be a man?'

He looked as surprised as she felt. 'Who are you suggesting, my lady? Not Emma? Surely she is too old and not experienced enough, though certainly she can give orders as well as any man I know.'

Her hands grew damp and she rubbed them down her *cyrtel*. Straightening her shoulders, Fayth met his gaze.

'I am suggesting myself, my lord.'

Chapter Seven

Giles's plan could not have gone better than this, for involving the lady had been his intent all along. Fearing that Fayth would refuse his request to do so, he'd dangled before her the duties that she'd carried out for her father over the last two years since her mother's passing. That information had come from Father Henry himself and was invaluable to understanding Lady Fayth.

And though everyone had called Edmund the earl's steward, Giles suspected that he held another position within Bertram's men, if any at all, and it was Fayth who in truth served her father as steward or chatelaine. Now was his chance to discover more about his new wife and the man who would have claimed her.

'I have worked at my father's side since I was but a small girl, my lord. I am organised and, though you believe me not, trustworthy in my efforts. More importantly, I seek only to protect my people…' He noticed her pause and wondered if her memory had lapsed and she'd forgotten who stood before her. Giles could almost hear the rest of it—*from you.*

'You have much to prove, lady,' he said, not yet agreeing though he knew he would. 'How do I know you will not aid Edmund and those who left with him to fight on another day?'

Giles sensed her yearning to be placed in charge and be in control of her people once more. He hoped his question and her claim of trustworthiness would force her to speak the truth, but sadness filled her gaze and she sighed once more.

'You cannot know because I do not know what I would do if put to that test, my lord. I am not certain I could withhold food from anyone starving, be they my people or yours or those who threaten our safety or those who tried to keep you out and now flee for their lives.' She sat back down in the chair and leaned her head against the pillow that cushioned the top edge. 'I cannot promise you that.'

He did not expect this turn in their discussions or for her to reject his offer. Convinced that she would indeed step into the position and aid his efforts, Giles had been overly confident and now faced failure. She'd surprised him once more.

'I am pleased at your candour, lady, and think it is easier to accept your confusion over the question than an answer given smoothly and without hesitation. We should both think on and consider this matter more before any decisions are made.'

Pray God that she'd told the truth about her in Edmund's plans and that she came to him a virgin and had tried to marry her father's man only in exchange for his help in avoiding Giles's claim. There could be so much between them if only he could trust her and trust her word. But, until she was proven or not, trust would have to wait.

'Come, seek your rest,' he said, holding his hand out to her.

'I will sleep here, my lord.' She began to lift the blanket up to her shoulders.

'Did I harm you last night while you slept?' He clenched his jaws together. She was a stubborn woman when she wanted to be.

'I did not sleep last night.'

He knew that. She'd never moved from her place against the wall. He'd listen to her breathing, which had never levelled into the pattern of sleep. The darkening skin around and beneath her eyes spoke of her exhaustion as well.

'We cannot be strong in the day without a night's good rest, lady.'

Meeting his gaze, Fayth knew this was about more than sleep. He was asking for her to believe his promises, ones that held not only dread but also a sense of anticipation for her. She did fear what would happen between them, but when she thought of the pleasure given by his kisses and his touch she wondered about the rest of it. Yet, the guilt of enjoying his touch struck her.

Catching sight of the ring that sat on her finger, she understood the bond between them and that, come sooner or come later, she would be his wife in truth and there was no way to avoid that day. It could be worse for her—her husband could have ravaged her and beaten her and kept her imprisoned for trying to take away what he believed was his legal claim to her and her lands. Others would surely have done so.

But not this Breton knight.

And mayhap if a sense of ease grew between them, she could discover the truth of her father's death and how this man had been given Taerford…and her. Accepting his hand, she stood and walked to the bed where he'd thrown the coverings open. Turning her back to him then, she reached up, gathered her hair in her hands and lifted it away from the neckline of her *cyrtel.*

'My lord?' Daring a glance over her shoulder, she noticed his surprise. 'I cannot untie the laces.'

He did not react for a few moments, but just as she began to ask once more she felt the touch of his fingers at her neck. The skin there tingled as he brushed her hair aside and tugged at the laces. She felt his hands move down her spine, pulling the laces free from her neck to her lower back. Her *cyrtel* opened then and the heat of his hands warmed her back as they moved ever lower.

Would he touch her again? It would be easy enough for him now that her *cyrtel* opened. She held her breath for a moment when he finished loosening the ties. He gripped each side of the dress and tugged at it to widen the gap more. And still she waited, holding her breath as her skin tingled and her stomach tightened in anticipation.

Giles pushed the kirtle forward, off her shoulders, and took a deep breath to release the tension growing within him. Allowing himself the weakness of one kiss, placed chastely on her neck, he fought the urge to slide his hands around her, to touch her breasts and tease the tips until they hardened, much as he was. There would be time and opportunity enough soon to touch her as he wished, and if her unashamed staring at him in the yard this morn gave any indication of her interest, she would allow it.

Soon.

His body reacted to the nearness of her, to the scent of some unnamed herb or flower that rose from her hair, to her exposed skin and the open shift. His male part hardened more, again, his loins ached and his mouth watered for all that her body offered. Shaking his head, he realised that he might have to add 'harlot' to his list of workers needed in Taerford if she did not prove her innocence soon.

Giles let his hands drop to his sides. He ignored the glances she cast, as though she'd expected him to do more, and waited for her to climb into the bed. He tried not to notice the thin gown she still wore or the way he could see her nipples pebbled against the fabric. He especially tried not to watch the way she crawled on hands and knees to the other side of the bed, giving him a view of her bottom that enticed and tempted him at once.

Before he could stop it, the image of her kneeling like that in front of him, with her hands placed against the wall, invaded his thoughts and another of him tossing up her gown and burying himself deep into the place between her legs burned itself into his mind. He would lean over her, hold those breasts in his hands, tease the nipples ever tighter and then thrust himself as far inside her as he could go. She would moan, for he would prepare her body first, using his mouth and tongue and hands and fingers, to make her hot and wet. And then he would mark her with his seed and his mouth so that every man would know that she was his alone.

Edmund and his plans be damned for she *would* be his alone!

Blinking his eyes, he found her under the many layers of coverings and settled on her back unlike last night. Before he could humiliate himself, he walked over to the table and poured wine into the goblet there. Drinking it down quickly and praying it would quench his newly built thirst and the hunger that raged through him, he waited for a few minutes in the quiet.

When his sense of control strengthened, Giles walked around the chamber putting out the few candles that still burned, placing the lady's shift on the chest, and then positioning his sword within easy reach beneath their pallet. Finally, lifting the top two layers on the bed and sitting on the edge of it, he unlaced his boots and tugged them off, tossing them nearby. Then his tunic and shirt and braies followed.

He climbed onto the bed, the ropes straining and giving, and lay on his back, listening as the entire keep settled for the night. After a long while, his body relaxed enough for him to feel sleep's pull. Lady Fayth breathed gently, as she had in the chair, and he contented himself with the thought that at least she would get some rest tonight.

However, now that he knew what delights lay beneath her clothing and that she was feeling some measure of curiosity about what would happen between them, there was no way to convince his male appendage that it would not happen. It was in the middle of that long, dark night when his body relented and sleep claimed him.

The shutters lay open when she woke in the morn and Fayth wondered when Giles had left the bed and the chambers. Her back did not ache though, a good sign, and she felt well rested. Sliding across the bed, she noticed the warmth yet remained on the place where he'd rested.

So, he'd preceded her to his duties by only a short time.

As soon as she began moving around the chamber, Emma entered bringing a pitcher of steaming water for her to wash. A few minutes later and she left the room, clean and dressed and in search of something meaningful to fill her day. As Fayth walked down the stairs to the hall the sound of voices reached her. Pausing, she listened to her husband and his friend argue over something.

Their location and the hushed voices spoke of their need for secrecy or, at the least, privacy. In a few minutes, she'd gathered that her husband was intent on a course of action that his friend believed to be the wrong one. They battled, with words and arguments, back and forth until the other one, Brice, cursed and stormed off. Giles remained in the stairwell and Fayth knew she must make her presence known or he would discover her.

She walked loudly back up a few steps and then down again, calling out to Emma as she did. When she turned and stood at the final flight of stairs, she acted surprised to see him there.

'Good day, my lord,' she said as she reached the place where he stood.

His eyes were still angry, she could tell, and he gritted his teeth as she noticed he did when agitated. Still, he took in and released a deep breath before addressing her.

'Lady,' he said, nodding to her. 'You look as though last night's sleep was better than the previous one.' Before she could speak, he tilted his head and stared at her. 'Ah, you heard Brice, then?'

'I could not understand all the words, but, yes, I heard you and your man arguing.' She'd decided on the truth. 'Is aught wrong? Has there been an attack?'

'Brice does not agree with my plan to allow you to act as steward here.'

Her breath caught at his statement. Did he truly mean to allow her to carry out those duties? Fayth had been certain that last night, when she could not promise not to aid those he deemed enemies, he'd decided to choose someone else. But now?

'Have you made up your mind, then, to accept his counsel in this?' she asked, following him down and onto the main floor.

'Just as you have little choice in your life, lady, I have little in mine. I need someone to take charge of our stores, our people and our preparations for the winter while I take control of the manor's defences and other protective measures. I could ask one of my men to step up to the task, but the one with the most experience in these matters is Stephen.'

He paused and watched her. Fayth gasped when she realised the identity of his man 'Stephen'—the soldier who'd hit her and nearly raped Ardith. None of her people would willingly help that man accomplish anything.

'I know that you punished him for his actions, but I am not certain that they have been forgotten.' The lump that yet remained on her scalp began to throb just at the memory of that encounter. She caught herself before lifting her hand to touch it.

'Just so, lady. Which is why I sought another instead of him. Have you given thought to my offer?' He glanced over to the large table where his trusted men sat waiting for him.

Fayth wanted to accept, but her heart was torn over this. Was it her role to act as her enemy's steward and help him retain his hold on her lands and people or should she be taking a more active stance and oppose this invader? Or should she do her best to keep her people strong so that they could overthrow this conqueror when Edmund and the others returned?

It was her custom to consult her father or Edmund over serious matters and her uncertainty over the correct path, but with them gone she had no one. And looking over at the new lord, standing a few feet away, stern-faced, arms crossed, already in his hauberk, she knew he would brook no delays and wanted her answer now.

'I will assist you in these duties, my lord.'

'Come, then,' he said, directing her to the table, 'there is much to do.'

With a pounding in her head and spasms in her back and arms, an exhausted Fayth sought her bed as soon as she finished eating. Her excitement at being given the authority to act lasted not much longer than it took her to greet the man who would oversee her in her duties— Brice. His enthusiasm for carrying out this favour for his friend waned with each passing hour and he questioned her every decision, her every conversation, even her every action.

Brice was as hard a taskmaster as she'd seen before, but if forced to it she would admit that his questions were fair ones, his doubts were ones she understood and his reactions were ones she'd seen in her father's actions. And, in spite of many prayers offered up during this day for patience and humility, it did not make it easier to accept.

Now, as she sank into the tub that Emma had waiting for her in her chambers, she questioned whether or not she was adequate to the position she'd accepted. Her legs ached from walking more in these last three days than she had in as many weeks. Reaching down to rub them clean made her arms and back ache even more. When she settled deeper into the hot water, she fought off sleep so that she could wash the sweat from her skin.

With Emma's help, she washed her hair and then climbed out, soon finding herself wrapped in drying cloths and sipping wine while Emma combed her hair before a well-stoked fire. Lulled nearly to sleep by the soothing motion and the feel of the comb running through her hair, Fayth closed her eyes. Unfortunately, her thoughts ran on in spite of her physical exhaustion. Lists of supplies. Lists of people. Lists of those missing. On and on it went until she decided that at the least her body could get some rest if she were in the bed. Dismissing Emma, she crawled under the covers and settled near the wall.

Something tugged at her thoughts, some aspect of her duties that was missing. She turned on her side, trying to ease the ache in her back as she realised the problem. She knew nothing of events and situations outside the walls of Taerford Manor. The new lord had not even permitted her outside the walls to the village yet and showed no signs of doing so.

Fayth thought on the tasks she must accomplish on the morrow and on how many she would need to assist her in them. Because of the need for the wall to be repaired and strengthened, Lord Giles had everyone who could work, and who was not assigned to other vital tasks, helping to cut down trees, bringing them inside the walls and chopping them into logs and planks to be used as they needed. Thus far, the only look to provisions he'd done were for those necessary for their daily food.

Most crops had been harvested and stored before the news had come of Harold Godwinson's first battle in the north with the forces of Harald Hardrada. When messengers had arrived with the news of their victory and then, on its heels, of their need to journey south to meet Duke William's army on the coast, her people had continued in their work, never believing that a foreign army could overpower the forces behind King Harold.

Not until word of the king's defeat and her father's death arrived had they thought to take any precautions about defending themselves from Norman incursions. Truly, at first, she had expected to hear that English forces had rallied and pushed the Norman duke back to the coast. Never dreaming that his forces would instead spread out down the Thames into the heart of Wessex, she'd carried on as her father would have expected her to.

His holdings, as Thane of Taerford, were modest enough to have tenants who paid him in crops and varied enough to support cattle, pigs and other crops. The mill on the river and the weavers brought additional coin to them to support all those who lived within his lands.

And now? She knew not how things would be now. Her husband spoke of such things only in hushed tones to his men, and truly only to a circle of a few—Roger, Matthieu, Lucien and Brice. Not to her. As though conjured by her thoughts, the door opened and Giles stepped in. He did not glance at the bed, only moved around the chambers quietly as though expecting her to be asleep…as she had these last two nights.

'I am awake, my lord,' she said, alerting him to her presence and wakefulness. Pushing up on her elbows, she nodded at the table. 'There is fresh wine if you would like some.'

Realising that he should be served it, Fayth lifted the covers and scrambled out. Her legs protested the quick move by cramping and she winced as she walked to the table. She filled a cup and turned to hand it to him.

His gaze did not stay on the wine; it might have paused there, but it settled on her breasts, exposed by the untied laces of the undergown. As the heated expression in his eyes grew stronger she grabbed both edges of the wayward gown and held them together. Lord Giles looked at her face then, but the heat did not diminish. Even after he swallowed the wine in one long draw, the desire in his expression did not lessen.

Her skin tingled as he reached out his hand towards her, gently pushing her own aside and touching her breasts through the thin linen layer. Her body pulsed with heat and a strange throbbing began between her legs, growing stronger as he slid his hands down and then up again over her. Breathing became difficult, for she kept holding it within her, waiting, waiting for something she could not name.

Giles stepped closer now and, deciding to move her boldly towards the passion he sensed she tried to control, spread the gown so that her breasts were open to his sight.

'Lovely,' he whispered in his Breton language. 'Beautiful,' he said, using his fingers to graze only the tips of them. When she trembled under his touch, he repeated it, enjoying the way her body responded to him.

His body reacted as well, his blood rushed through his veins, readying him to join hers. Every encounter threatened his decisions about her and he knew he was not ready to take her in that final way. Ready? *Oui.* Not willing was more the case. Giles then used his whole hand to cup each of her breasts, holding them, caressing the tips with his thumbs as he moved his hands under their fullness and soft skin.

She let out a sigh and her eyes closed then, only for a moment, but there was a softening in her gaze when she opened them once more. He took advantage of that moment to move to her side, still touching her, still caressing her breasts, and then to stand behind her. Now, he encircled her with his arms and continued to enjoy the feel of her in front of him, against him, just near him. When his cock rose to fullness between them, she did not startle, and he held her tighter to savour the feel of it.

Fayth would tell herself later that she did not resist because she was exhausted or because she feared angering him, but the shameful reason was that pleasure overwhelmed her. If her mother or Emma had revealed that a simple touch could bring about such myriad feelings and cause her body to heat as though on fire, she would not have believed it.

Now, feeling her body tighten and ache with his every touch and feeling it throb each time he whispered his foreign words in that husky, deep voice, she knew he did this with a purpose in mind. Lord Giles was seducing her, much as any lord could or would seduce a maiden into giving away her favours. The only way she could justify this and explain her weakness was their marriage vows and his right to claim her.

As her body responded to him she felt as though she would fall, her legs trembled beneath her, so she leaned back against him for support. He surprised her by accepting her weight and shifting his arms to hold her closely. Fayth felt the presence of his manhood between them and allowed herself to lean back against him and it. He pushed forward once and then again and then rested it there without moving it.

She thought he was done exploring her body as was his right when he released her breast and used his free hand to push her hair aside. Nuzzling her neck, he laid kisses along the line of her shoulder up to her neck and then caught the edge of her ear with his teeth. She shook then, uncontrollably, and she heard his soft laughter as it vibrated against her skin. Did this please him in some way? Too far into pleasure to consider more, she allowed him his way.

She was soft. She trembled in his embrace. She did not stop him. Giles slid his hand down from her hair and grasped the thin gown, gathering it in his hand and exposing her legs now to his gaze and his touch. At first, she reached down and covered his hand with hers, he thought to stop him from his obvious intent, but then she just let hers remain there on his while he moved ever lower.

The mass of soft curls guarding the junction of her thighs tickled his palm but his body screamed for more than a touch. Without thinking, he arched against her, rubbing his straining cock against her bottom and savouring the explosion of pleasure it caused. Lady Fayth moved within his arms then, closer to him and with more pressure on his hand, guiding him forward on his quest.

Her panting breaths changed then and he realised she held her breath. As did he. He spread his fingers wide and touched the curls gently at first, just barely grazing them and then running his fingers along them with more pressure and then slipping between her legs to touch the centre of her excitement.

Her body might be inexperienced at this but it wept onto his fingers as he touched that intimate place and slid along the folds of her womanhood. She shook in his arms and he shifted his other arm to hold her more firmly against him and he continued to caress her. He knew what he searched for and he touched and rubbed her, making her gasp over and over again until he found it—the tiny budlike nub.

Giles rubbed there until he felt another gush of wetness from deeper within and then, spreading it along the folds, he caressed every inch he could reach. Sliding one, then two, then three fingers inside and drawing them out, he used it to ease his path and to heighten her pleasure. She tossed her head where she leaned it on his chest and Giles began to kiss her neck, licking and nipping it in time with his fingers down there.

Then, when he felt her body tighten and prepare for that final step of release, he took the nub between his finger and thumb and rolled it there. Squeezing there and still sliding over it, he felt her entire body shake and she began to moan.

'Giles?' she murmured through clenched teeth. 'Giles?' she asked again on a breathy moan.

'Do not fear this, my lady. Do not fear,' he repeated as he leaned down and kissed and used his teeth on her neck in a place that seemed to be a sensitive one to her. With his mouth there and his fingers rubbing the engorged folds and nub between her legs, his name was now an announcement rather than a question.

'Giles!'

Her body shook now and he held her tightly as tremors moved through her. Fayth could not stop herself from arching into his hand or from rubbing herself against his touch at a faster pace than the one he moved to. And she could not stop herself from pressing her bottom against his hardness.

Wave after wave of pleasure struck her, making it difficult to breathe and impossible to think of anything except his fingers rubbing in and against that most private place. Losing any remnant of control, she released herself into his power and let the aching and the answering pleasure escalate until it flowed throughout her body. She might have screamed, but she did not care or know at that moment.

A few moments or minutes later, she gained a sense of herself and found herself collapsed against her husband and him against the wall. Not remembering when that had occurred or when he had removed his fingers from that place, she tried to lift her head and move away. He held her tightly and thrust against her once and then twice and then his body shook. The place between them and the back of her under-gown dampened as he released his seed there. With a loud exhalation, he rested his head against her shoulder and she felt his heated breaths against her skin.

Confused and feeling very vulnerable in his embrace, she pushed free and stood there, unable to face him. How could something so wondrous occur between enemies? How could she respond to his touch as she had? This was different from helping her people and aiding him as a result. This was a personal betrayal of her father's memory.

And, in spite of knowing that, her body yet throbbed as small waves of pleasure pulsed through her, duller each time, but a reminder of her weakness.

Giles mumbled something behind her, whether in his tongue or badly spoken English she knew not, and then he stepped farther away, opening one of the chests that lined the wall with her clothing in it. Handing it to her without looking at her, he remained turned away while she gathered the soiled gown and pulled it over her head, replacing it with the clean one before climbing back into the bed. A heaviness now lay on her heart and she could do nothing but pray it would lift.

She heard him walking around the chamber, preparing for the coming night, and she waited for him to climb in next to her. Turning on her side away from him, she allowed the tears that had threatened for days to flow now, in silence, for all that she had lost and still stood to lose in the coming months.

Chapter Eight

'What the hell did you do to her?' Brice whispered furiously, his voice kept low so others would not hear. Giles's friend looked around to make certain no one stood near and then repeated his question. 'What happened between you?'

'Nothing happened, Brice. Now see to your duties,' Giles ordered, hoping Brice would take his hint and stop asking anything more.

'She looks like a dog that's been kicked down, Giles. She did not even rise to my bait as we broke our fast. She has done nothing but insult my intelligence, my plans and my actions these last days since you asked me to watch over her and the work she does for you. And this morn, she arrives at table and will not even meet my eyes.' Brice glared at him. 'Nor yours.'

When Giles tried walking around him, Brice stepped the other way and blocked him there. 'What did you do, my lord Taerford?'

Giles huffed out a breath and looked heavenward, praying for patience in dealing with his friend. 'I pleasured her,' he admitted.

Brice crossed his arms over his chest and narrowed his gaze, watching Giles's expression. 'Against her will?'

'Nay! I would do no such thing.'

'And the problem lies...where?' Brice asked, probing as a healer dug at a splinter.

'She cried.'

Giles shook off his hold and walked out into the yard. There was much to do today and he really did not have the time to waste worrying over a woman's tears in their marriage bed. He had not even forced himself on her and yet... yet. Brice caught up with him and they walked towards the stables.

'I thought you were not going to bed her until you know if she is breeding or not?'

'I did not,' he answered. 'But this was a simple bit of...?' He could not think of the phrase so he waved Brice off. 'I did not hurt her.'

'Did you frighten her?'

That question brought him to a halt. Was that the problem? Had the response of her body to his touches and kisses frightened her? If so, did that mean she was innocent? Certainly she was inexperienced, that much was clear to him. He would swear on his mother's soul that what had happened to her last night, under his hand, had been the first time she'd reached sexual release.

He glanced over at his friend, who stood waiting for his answer as though she were under his protection. 'I may have. But why is this of concern to you? Have you nothing better to do with your time here than to plague me with questions about my bedplay?' He crossed his arms and glared at his friend. 'I wish Soren was here now for he could entertain you with stories of his exploits and you would leave me in peace over this.'

'You asked for my help to watch over your wife, Giles, and to discover if she is still in league with Edmund. Work with her, you said. Judge her worthiness, you said. Discover if she is a traitor to you or a spy for your enemies, you said. I do not do this for the amusement, my lord. The work of a reeve and steward are more than I wish to do.' Brice crossed his arms over his chest matching Giles's own stance and glared back.

Truly, though Brice did not serve him, he had been invaluable during the attack to chase the rebels from Taerford and in these first few weeks of trying to organise the people and lands now his. He but waited on the king's word and the king's men to continue on to what would become his fief, Thaxted, in the north. And they both waited on news of Soren's recovery from his battle wounds.

'Your pardon, my friend. I did ask for your help. And your service has been very useful to me. It is just that this is a private matter, between the lady and myself.' He realised the falseness of his words as soon as he said them.

'Not learned that lesson yet, have you, my friend?' Brice replied sarcastically.

And, as if to prove the point, the very subject of their discussion made her way out into the yard and towards where they stood, stopping along the way to speak to some of the men working there. The part that made Brice's point in the argument again was the way everyone there looked first to the lady and then at him and back to her again. It seemed they all thought her in some way injured or mistreated…by him. He looked at Brice and hung his head in surrender.

Brice clapped him on the back. 'Their lady is an innocent, raised amongst them and the one thing standing between them and their new invading Norman lord,' he began.

'Breton,' he corrected.

'It matters not to these people. She stands for them and you rejected her on your wedding night.'

'I did not reject her,' he tried to explain, but Brice stopped him.

'You have not bedded her and they know it. But you gave them hope when first you saw to their protection and then when you asked for her help. They believe that they could survive with you. Now, this morn, they only know that something ill transpired between the two of you and they take her side.' Looked at from that eye, Brice was correct.

'I think it will take no more than a week before I know for certain. Either the lady bleeds or…'

'She approaches now.' Brice turned to her. 'Have you told her that you are leaving?'

'Nay. Though I wish to see her mood lighten, I have no wish to see the joy in her expression at the news.'

Brice laughed then, long and hearty, drawing attention.

'You will not find the transition from foreign bastard knight to lord an easy one either, Brice. I wish I could be there to see how you fare when faced with these very same problems.'

'I intend to learn from your errors, Giles.' Brice nodded to the lady. 'Do you seek me or your lord husband, Lady Fayth?' he asked in a louder voice.

She came to stand before him and yet did not raise her eyes to meet his. 'I did not know if you had asked Lord Giles for permission to go to the village, sir,' she said to Brice.

'Why do you wish to go to the village, lady?' Giles asked. 'You can speak your request to me.'

Her veil covered her head and her hair and

wrapped around her neck, keeping everything he liked most from his view. He realised that this Saxon clothing covered its women from head to toe, showing little difference in a stout figure like Emma's or a slender one like the lady's. Mayhap Simon's wife could be prevailed upon to send some of the dresses she wore to Fayth? The more form-fitting style appealed to him.

He brought his gaze back to the veil, for it was all he could see of her until she raised her head a little. The white fabric also brought out the dark circles still under her eyes. At least she would sleep well while he was gone these next few days.

'I, we, my lord, have taken inventory of all supplies and foodstuffs in the keep and the other manor buildings, but my father stored much of the produce, wool and weaving in the village. I need to go there to…'

He watched her as she spoke but all he thought of was the night before when she'd writhed under his touch. He wanted to see the flush of sexual arousal on her cheeks and to see the way her eyes gleamed when she cried out her release. He wanted to see her smile once more.

'Brice can do that,' he offered, now concentrating on her words and not his fantasies.

Brice's continued glare told him of his failure to do it well. The lady was more valuable than all of the supplies or stores in the keep and village and he could not afford to let her out of the safety of the keep's walls. 'I would not have you exposed to the dangers outside these walls, lady. I want you to stay here until my return.'

Fayth did look up then, startled by his words. 'You are leaving, my lord?'

'*Oui*. Aye. The king has granted me lands and I must ride the borders to see the extent of them. The map I have is only the most rudimentary and tells me nothing of their conditions or uses.'

'I could tell you that, my lord. I have ridden these lands since I was a child.' He did not know if her offer was to help or to keep him from going out onto the lands beyond the manor and village.

'The king granted me your father's lands and more, lady. My property includes eighty hides of land.'

She gasped at the size of it, for it was more than double her father's property. 'But Lord Leofwyne owns the land to the north and east of these lands,' she said, shaking her head.

'He fell in battle, lady. His lands are forfeit to the duke.' Giles had spoken the words softly, but their effect was as though trumpeted throughout the keep. She paled before him.

'How many others? How many Saxons were killed by your Duke William?' she cried out. She'd only just begun to think on such things, lost in her own battle not to accept the pleasure he offered, but now, with his declaration about the extent of his reward for battle service, she needed to know.

He grimaced before answering her, so she knew the number would shock her. His expression became flat, his eyes dull and his lips tightened in a thin line across his face.

'Close to four thousand, lady. So far as could be told, all of Godwin's sons. Harold's house-carls fought at his side and perished. The great earls of Mercia, Sussex, Wessex, Kent and East Anglia. Many more that I cannot put a name to.'

His voice carried no gloating tone and she thought she could hear sympathy in his words and that surprised her. 'And their lands and people are given away?'

'The duke has the right,' he began, but then he stopped and did not try to justify the actions.

Fayth could not comprehend the amount of devastation caused by this single battle, except that life in England was changed for ever by it. Her stomach churned at the thought of never seeing uncles, cousins and other kin again. And how did the women fare without their men to provide for and protect them? Surely not all Saxon lords had daughters to use to legitimise the gifts from the duke and to cement the invaders to their conquered peoples.

From Edmund's words, she believed that many Saxon lords still lived and were gathering in the north to push the Normans out of their country. He mentioned that the *witan* voted Edgar the Atheling as king and that support was growing throughout England for him.

Horrified that she'd been sitting here, safe in the keep and succumbing to the pleasures of the flesh with this man while not knowing the truth of her people's, the Saxons', fate shamed her. And not being brave enough to face her captor, be he husband or not, and to find out filled her with resolve. Her shame became her strength and she asked the question that had haunted her days and nights. The one that would either give her hope or ruin any chance of living in peace with her husband.

'Did you kill my father to gain these lands?'

Giles knew no good answer to her question, but he would not lie to her in this matter either. He'd like to, especially since her face now grew deathly pale, very different from the recent glow that was taking hold there. She clutched her hands so tightly before her that they grew white from lack of blood.

'I may have, lady.' He ran his hand through his hair and looked away for a moment as a certain despair filled him. 'I may have.'

When she stumbled and would have fallen, he stepped next to her and put his arm around her waist to support her. She would have pulled free, but he held her easily and began walking towards the keep with her.

'Brice, call all who were high in Lord

Bertram's regard or held places of honour at his table to the hall.' Before Brice could question his intentions, he called out again. 'Bring any of Lord Bertram's men-at-arms who remain in my service there as well. Send word to the village for those who owed service to the old lord to come now to the keep.'

He did not slow his pace, but held on to the lady and half carried her with him. He cursed himself for not handling this as soon as he'd taken control, but he had believed it was not necessary. Now, he could see in hindsight that it was far too late. Giles had thought to protect the lady from the harsh realities wrought by this war and the one her king had fought just before it, but he must right the effects of that faulty decision.

Entering the keep from the back, he continued on through to the hall, gathering a crowd of those working as he dragged their lady with him. Reaching the large table, he pulled out one of the chairs and placed her in it. Crouching in front of it, he took her chin in his fingers and turned her so that she faced him.

'Lady?' When she did not meet his gaze, he shook her face gently and spoke again. 'Fayth?'

This time when she did look at him the grief and pain there were nearly too much for him to gaze upon.

'I do not know if your father fell under my sword or my bow. In battle it is sometimes impossible to know.'

Tears filled her eyes again and she blinked several times before replying. 'And is that to soothe my conscience or yours, my lord?' she asked in an empty voice.

'Neither,' he said with a shrug. 'A warrior reconciles himself to the necessities of war before he enters. No man goes into battle or war without knowing that he will cause many deaths even as someone else tries to cause his. I simply tried to tell you the truth.'

Noticing the people gathering in the hall, he stood back and ordered Emma to see to her lady. He watched as the maid forced her to drink a sip of wine and then called Roger to his side to explain his intentions. Roger accepted his orders and left to arrange the men as he'd directed. Brice…Brice stood as always at his back whether he agreed or not with his decision.

Giles accepted a cup of wine from one of the servants and thought over the words he would use to set out his plans for Taerford and its people.

Edmund gave the signal to hold. Something was amiss here.

As they watched from the cover of the forest the Normans began rounding up all the villagers and herding them to the keep.

It was rushed.

It was forced and no one was permitted to remain behind.

Not a good sign of the new lord's intentions.

'What do you think he is doing?' William asked.

Edmund watched as the villagers made their way down the road to the keep, their fear evident in the way they walked and the glances they threw back at their homes. Would Edmund and his men be betrayed to the Norman? Many were aware of their excursions into the village to seek supplies that Edmund knew were stored there, but would any of them reveal that knowledge?

He dared not move closer now; the absence of most of the villagers would not shield such movements. With a wave and signal, he led his men back through the forest, along the river to their camp.

He'd hoped to get word about Fayth for he'd not heard much of her welfare until just days before. Apparently injured during the attack and kept prisoner in her chambers until just five days ago, she had been forced to the chapel by the Norman and taken in marriage against her will. Edmund could only imagine the perversions forced on Lord Bertram's innocent daughter by the Norman knight who claimed her and her lands.

The one who'd killed Lord Bertram at Hastings.

Once he spoke to the leaders of the other troops and received word from King Edgar, he would come up with a plan to rescue the lady... and bring her to his side. Through her, he could reclaim the lands that should be his, the lands

Bertram had promised him if he kept Fayth safe from the invading forces.

And whether, in the end, he decided to take her in marriage himself or give her to a faithful vassal, removing her foreign husband would be the easiest part of the plan.

They'd travelled only a few miles towards their camp when a man reached them with the news that the villagers were back and all alive and apparently well. Curious to discover what had happened, Edmund ordered his men back towards Taerford village.

Chapter Nine

Giles's every nerve jangled as he watched them assemble before him. A glance at the lady did nothing to settle him for Fayth grew even paler as her people gathered there. Giles suspected she worried that he would have them killed, but for now he would say nothing else to her about his plans. All of his people would hear his words at the same time.

Nothing in his life, nothing learned at Sir Gautier's knee or on the many battlefields, had prepared him for this moment, but he gained strength from knowing that he could do well by these people even as he prospered from them. He knew that Duke William supported him in this endeavour and that the duke would never give up his claim to England and these lands. With that backing and his own plans and desires for success, Giles would make his stand and his claim.

Roger called out his name and every person quieted.

'In defeating your king and your lord in battle, Duke William has made his claim on this land. By right of battle and with the pope's blessing, England is his and the lands held by those who fought at Harold's side are forfeit.'

Loud grumbling went through the crowd and Giles waited for it to pass.

'In supporting his liege lord, Bertram of Taerford risked his life and lands and, with his defeat and death, his lands and more have been given to me. My liege lord requested only one sign of fealty from me for this bestowal—that I marry the old lord's daughter. I have done that before you as witnesses.' He watched as, to a one, they glanced over at Fayth.

'These lands are mine now, held in trust with the duke who will be crowned King of England,' he called out loudly. Then, in a lower voice, he said, 'And she is mine.'

Her gaze met his in that moment and he did not look away. Something heated and alive passed between them then and his body ached for the moment he would claim her and make her his in truth. She would know his possession of her body soon, but he wanted her and those watching to know that, in fact, she was his even now, regardless of the consummation or not of their vows.

'She is mine,' he repeated more forcefully. Giles watched as she shivered at his proclamation, revealing that she was affected even now.

'The men who tried to keep me from my rightful claim are outlaws now, rebels against the lawful ruler of England, and will suffer if captured.' He walked closer to them and laid his hand on the sword at his side.

'Make no mistake, I will not allow these men to take what is mine and I will not allow them to harm anything of mine. I know that many are kinsmen or have lived amongst you here in Taerford and I would rather not put them to the sword.'

Giles looked around at the people and then back at Fayth as he now crossed his arms over his chest.

'But force my hand and I will.'

He waited as they considered his words and warning. Declaring a man to be an outlaw was a death sentence for they could be killed without hesitation or fear of punishment under the law. Anyone helping an outlaw could be exiled themselves and lose everything they possessed. A man's family could be thrown out of their home and off any lands they owned or rented if outlawed—a death sentence even if not called such. This was the same in Brittany as here and they knew it. He watched as they accepted his warning of the consequences of helping those outlawed by their own behaviour.

He turned to face the villeins gathered together in one part of the hall. 'I will honour the agreements for land and rents that you had with Lord Bertram until next year.'

Facing those who served the lord and belonged to the manor, he said, 'I bind you and your service to me, even as you served Lord Bertram. I offer you my protection within the keep or without, as long as you honour your bond to me.'

The last group of men stood together probably out of long practice. Some of Bertram's men-at-arms had been injured or had stayed behind protecting the keep or the lady and, when faced with his superior force of mounted soldiers and bowsmen, had surrendered to Giles at the onset of fighting.

'For now, my men will see to the manor's defences and you need to continue at your labours until the preparations for winter are complete. Then you may train with my men and learn from them.

'I would ask those who fought for pay to pledge to me now and I will honour those arrangements. Those who had pledged to Lord Bertram may pledge their fealty to his daughter.'

He heard Roger call out in disagreement and felt Brice's approach from behind. He stayed them with a hand in the air. 'As I am also pledged to the lady in honour and in marriage, I have no objections to her father's men pledging their honour to her as well.'

Fayth could not believe his words. By right, as lord, he could have imprisoned the soldiers for not swearing to him. He could have had them executed. Instead, he asked them to pledge to her? Unable to speak and nearly unable to breathe, she watched as every one of those who fought in her father's name knelt before them and lowered their heads, a sign of respect and obeisance.

The silence in the hall was profound as he held out his hand to her. Accepting it, she rose to stand at his side, not quite knowing what to expect of him in that moment. He drew her closer to him and then walked forward to stand in front of the kneeling men.

'Do you give your word to honour your pledge of duty to me as your lord?' he asked. At their pledge, he moved before those of her father's men who knelt. 'Do you give your word to me that you will honour your pledge of duty to the lady, Fayth Fitzhenry, daughter of Bertram of Taerford?'

He was showing a great deal of intelligence for one she'd thought so unpractised in the arts of nobility, for many would think it was his unfamiliarity with her language that caused the slight change in the words he chose for their promise to him. Fayth noted it and suspected the clear purpose behind it. She almost smiled at the way he skilfully worded the question, making the men answerable to him in their duties to her.

The men cheered their pledge, calling out her name and she did smile then, in pride and honoured by their promises to her. Lord Giles continued as she thought he would, calling those who had just pledged forward to hear their name and take their hand. When each had been greeted by name, he spoke again, bringing them to quiet.

'It will be very hard to carry on our duties while there is unrest and turmoil surrounding us, but we must or we will not survive. There will be disputes between Norman and Saxon, there will be disagreements to settle and many difficulties to face, but we can persevere in this.'

At first no one spoke or made a noise and she could see the disappointment on the lord's face. He believed he had gained support from her people, and so did she, so this silence was disheartening. Then, one of the men, Norman or Saxon she knew not which, called out his name and it spread through the hall. He accepted their gesture for a few moments and then dismissed them back to their work.

She would have left, but he still held her hand, effectively keeping her at his side. Fayth watched Roger and some of the other knights lead the villeins out. The others who worked with the manor walls went back to their duties, just as she should.

'My lord,' she said softly, interrupting his words with Brice. 'I should return to my duties as well.'

Instead of releasing her, he shook his head and escorted her back to the chair next to the table in the front of the hall, dismissing his friend with but a glance. He pulled a stool over and sat before her.

'Are you well now, lady?'

'I am…not.' There was no way to explain what was in her heart to him—that no matter his rights under the law, she felt as though she was betraying her father when she enjoyed his attentions. And the pleasure he'd shown her in their bed only worsened her feelings of betrayal.

'I think I have distressed you. Last evening, I

had sought to ease your fears by showing you how enjoyable it can be between a man and a woman, but the result has been the opposite of what I had hoped. Now, today, I sought to reassure you that there is a future for our people.'

His words did not calm her but instead she could feel a torrent of emotions and words bursting forward. Her hands shook and she clasped them together in her lap. It was all she could control in that moment of recklessness.

'Ease my fears, my lord? Was that your goal, then?' she whispered furiously. She stood then and faced him. 'You all but admitted your part in my father's death. You still believe that I gave up my honour. Do you think I would come willingly to you when I believe you would imprison me in the blink of an eye if I do not prove to be innocent? Oh, but wait, I have come to you, haven't I?'

She drew in a breath then, somehow unable to stop now that this dam of self-control had burst within her.

'I sleep in your bed and even lie beneath your touch and gain pleasure from it. And all the while you make no promises of mercy if I do carry a child now. Would you give it to some convent or villager to raise and then take your pleasure on me, breeding sons of your own?' Surprise showed on his face at her words. 'Do you fear raising another man's bastard or only fear raising a Saxon's?'

Fayth knew the moment she'd crossed some line with him, for his eyes burned and his face grew hard. He stood up so quickly that he sent the stool flying across the room and against the wall with a crash. Fayth backed away several steps but he crossed the distance with but one of his paces. Brice came between them, whispering to him in their language. So fast were the words that she stood no chance of gaining an understanding of them.

Before Giles could explode, as the fury in his eyes foretold, she stumbled away and ran from the table. Terrified by the expression of absolute rage on his face, she ran out of the keep, across the yard to the stone chapel. Pushing the door open and closing it behind her, she scrambled down the aisle to the front. Knowing there was no place to hide, she made her way to the half wall that separated the altar from the rest of the chapel and sat down in front of it.

Or rather she collapsed against it, for her legs gave out on her then. Sitting there, she did nothing until her heart ceased to pound within her chest and until she could breathe without tightness.

How foolish she'd been! She'd made good steps these last few days in organising the keep, but her doubts last night, being pleasured by this invader and enjoying his touch, had raged full this day until she overstepped herself. Where was her self-control?

Even as he confirmed her place and importance to him and the people, she undermined it. Instead of keeping her doubts to herself, she'd lashed out at him. And other than tempting her to passion, what had been his sins?

She did not diminish his part in the battle between her king and his duke, but, as he said, he fought for his liege as her father had. Fayth shifted on the cold stone floor. It was as men were and would ever be—fighting for honour and lands and power. With so much land to divide up amongst those who followed and fought well with him, the duke would give lands to men who could be good-hearted or cold-hearted in their treatment of their new subjects.

Fayth knew, after watching him proclaim his rights and those of her people, that he was a better lord than most. The promises he'd made today were ones that her father would have made and honoured if he were alive. And with her emotional reaction and inability to accept him for his own actions, she'd ruined any respect growing between them.

She sat there for a long time, pondering what she'd done and her feelings about her place in this Norman's, nay Breton's, keep, when the door that led to the priest's small room opened and Father Henry entered. Fayth would have stood then if she could have, but her legs would not move. The priest bowed at the altar, spent a few moments in prayer and then turned to her.

'Are you well, child?' he asked, holding his hand out to her.

'Nay, Father, I am heartsick and unwell, I fear,' she answered, waving off his hand. He was not a strong man and she feared that they would both end up on the cold stone floor if she took it.

'I miss your father as well, Fayth.' He smiled at her and she feared breaking out into tears again at the warmth and concern there. 'You are a strong person, my dear. You will survive this ordeal.'

'I try to be a daughter my father would be proud of,' she explained. 'But…' She paused, unable to say the rest.

'It was easier to be your father's daughter when he was here to advise and guide you? When it meant following his rules and obeying his commands?'

'Yes, that is it, Father. Now there is no one to counsel me on matters big or small. I have no one now,' she whispered.

Father Henry reached for her again and this time he would brook no refusal. He steadied her as she stood and straightened her gowns and veil. 'He would listen to your questions and give you good counsel, lady.'

Had grief made his thoughts addled? she wondered. Surely, Father Henry did not think her father could speak to her now. 'He, Father? Who do you mean?'

'He,' Father said with a nod towards the back of the chapel. 'Lord Giles came to me and asked me to see to your welfare.' She did not look behind to see him. 'He said he had frightened you badly with his anger and did not wish for you to be fearful of him.'

'He told you that?' she asked in a whispered voice, still not looking back.

'Yes, my dear. I think he is a good man, lady. I see much of your father at that age in him. I think you could trust him.'

'You do?' Fayth was shocked by Father Henry's confidence in this new lord.

'Yes. He may make mistakes in his struggles here, but he is willing to correct them. Not like many Normans, eh? And you are his lawful wife now. Your place is beside him, whether your father chose him or some other did so in his stead.'

A kind way of saying what had happened, but it was the truth, however phrased. Still her larger question was one she could not speak of with Father Henry. Or could she?

'Father, but do I betray those lost by being his wife?' She would never speak of the fleshly passion between them to this priest, but she needed his counsel.

'Lady, you spoke the words joining yourself to him in this very chapel. For whatever reasons, you consented to this marriage and are now his wife.' He pulled her closer and lowered his voice then. 'And if there is some pleasure gained when carrying out the duties of wife with your lord husband, I am sure the Good Lord does not frown on such. And neither will I,' he assured her.

Tears filled her eyes as she heard the words he spoke and she reached up to wipe them away.

'So, child, will you speak to him or should I send him away?' Father Henry stood straighter then and nodded once more towards the back of the chapel.

Unless she decided to seek refuge in the chapel for the rest of her days, Fayth knew she must face her husband and come to some understanding if there was to be peace between them. That he would go to the priest and ask him to intercede was remarkable and, again, something she suspected most of the other Norman noblemen would not waste their time doing when force in any measure would accomplish things even faster. It had been reports of just such atrocities that had made her consent to marriage with Edmund.

'I will speak to him, Father,' she said quietly.

'Good, child. Let me escort you to him.'

Father Henry held out his arm and Fayth placed her hand there, using a small bit of his strength to steady herself as she walked to Giles.

'My lord,' Father began, 'would you like to use the chapel for your discussion? The presence of God can be most helpful in such situations.' Before Lord Giles could answer, Father Henry walked off and pulled two chairs to the centre of the chapel. Setting them up to face each other, he nodded and smiled.

'My lord,' he said, pointing to one chair. 'My lady,' he said, helping her to sit on the other one.

Her stomach churned again as she sat and waited for him to speak. But it was Father Henry who interrupted first.

'I could stay with you, if you'd like, my lord?'

She did smile then, for she knew, as Lord Giles and Father Henry did, that the priest was not asking him, but her, if she wished his presence.

'Lady?' Giles asked her softly. 'Would you wish Father Henry to stay?' He added an inflection to the priest's name that made it sound more French than English.

'Nay, my lord. I am certain he has other tasks to see to and would not detain him here.'

Father Henry bowed to them and then made his way to the altar where he spent a few moments in prayer before leaving. When she dared to look at her husband, she saw not the raging man but the one to whom she'd grown accustomed. When Father Henry had left, she heard Giles take a deep breath in and let it out loudly.

'So, lady, would you like to know the truth about the man you have to husband?'

Chapter Ten

Giles looked at Fayth who looked certain about very little at this moment and whose face still wore its pale colour and whose eyes still filled with fear. And frightened she should be, for he had nearly lost control and raised his hand to her when she had insulted him in the hall. But for Brice's timely intervention, Giles suspected he might have taken a step from which he could never return.

He had never raised a hand to any woman, nor servant, in his life, though he'd been on the receiving end of that many times. He did not shy away from the application of discipline when needed, but it was never done in anger. Now, trying to be calm and rational, he wondered what it was about her that made him lose control—of his anger this day, but of his lust last eventide and the night of their marriage. In the cold, glaring light of day, he made decisions and then, in the dark of night, when faced with the woman in his bed, he lost his mind.

'Brice said that I cannot hold you responsible for an insult if you do not know how you did it,' he said to begin.

'I offered insult simply by voicing my accusations, my lord. That would be enough for most men to strike out.' She sighed then and gazed at him with tear-filled eyes. 'I feel like these last days have been a waking nightmare for me—one in which I've lost control and can do nothing right or well,' she said.

Did she know she mirrored his own feelings? Although he suspected that his lack of control was in part due to her appeal to him, physically and for all that she offered him.

'I think part of your fear is from not knowing what is happening outside our walls. Change has come to England on swift horses and it is stopping for no one.'

'But you seem to embrace it, my lord,' she said, leaning forward and meeting his gaze once more.

'Ah, but I stand to benefit more than most from these changes, while you, you and your people, stand to lose the most.'

'So, Father Henry said I should seek your counsel. Will these truths you mentioned aid me in ridding myself of fear or increase it?'

He stood then and walked a few steps away. 'I am not certain if you will be comforted by what I have to say or if it will make things worse between us, lady.'

Giles watched as indecision flitted across her face. Father Henry had spoken of her courage and her strength of spirit, from her mother he'd said, but Giles waited to see it once more.

She drew in a ragged breath and nodded. 'Tell me your truths, husband.'

'I am not noble born, lady. Indeed, my birth was baseborn—my father is a vicomte and my mother a weaver serving on one of his father's estates.'

'So that is why you serve yourself?' she asked.

'Just so. A bastard makes his own way in the world and even servants look askance at his requests.'

'And why you have no manservant to see to your needs.'

'Also that. A knight needs no one to see to him except to care for his armour and his horses.'

'And why you are not comfortable with everyone knowing your every move and word.'

'I had no idea you were so observant, lady.' Or had he been so obvious to everyone else? He began to pace around the chairs.

'I had only taken notice last evening, my lord. 'Tis why I got out of bed to serve you your wine.'

Her face blushed then, in memory no doubt of what serving him wine had led them to. He would not pursue that topic now.

'Other than watching it from my place down the table in my father's house, I am not experienced in all of the pomp and ceremony expected by a lord. I do not know that I ever will be.' He smiled at her then. 'At least the duke had the good sense to make me only a baron. A baron is not high enough to worry over all the pretensions of rank. We are still close enough to the ground to keep our feet there.'

'So, is your duke favouring those of his warriors who faced the same challenges as he?'

He laughed then, at her scrupulously polite manner of calling the duke a bastard. He was, and everyone knew it, he revelled in it and used it to tweak the noses of those he wished to insult. But few made it away unscathed if they used it to insult him.

He'd suspected that William had been attempting to raise up a few deserving men who'd begun life as he had, but upon investigating the locations of their awarded demesnes and the proximity to Godwin's supporters' holdings, he was beginning to think there were other issues at play.

'I am beginning to wonder if just the opposite might be true, lady. The three of us given lands to hold if we could take them are all bastards of noble men who were trained together with my half brother in my uncle's holdings in Rennes. I begin to suspect that we are expendable to the duke or his nobles.'

'That is outrageous,' she said. 'To use you like that is...' She did not finish the sentence.

'Extremely practical actually. We three hold

no lands and have no powerful allies at home who would be outraged—' he nodded to her as he used her word '—at our deaths in taking or holding these lands. In fact, I believe that all of the nobles holding lands around this and the other grants have legitimate heirs who could take over at any moment for us.'

Why had they not been aware of this before? Probably because he and Brice had been too busy seeing to Soren's care and too over-whelmed by the news of the grants to look too closely at the reasons behind it. It had been questionable in that first week if Soren would survive the blow that came after the surrender was called. Even now he remained behind, re-cuperating and gaining strength while waiting for the duke's troops to move northward after taking control of the south.

'You mentioned three, my lord? Dare I guess that Brice is included in the duke's largesse?' she asked.

He laughed then. 'Do you think him ex-pendable after being forced to work with him these last days?'

She smiled then and Giles saw a glimpse of

the beauty she could be when her face lit with pleasure. 'Though I would never say this before him, and pray that you will not reveal it to him, he seems to want only your good and pursues it without delay. He stands ever at your back. Has it always been thus?'

'*Oui.* Aye. And Soren as well. I hope you meet him.' The words were out of his mouth and he shook his head denying them. 'Nay! He has an appeal to women that none can match. After he claims his land and marries, then I will let him visit here.'

Now she laughed. 'He worries you so?'

'Women flock to his side, lady. He never sleeps alone for want of a woman.'

'I shall remember that if he visits, my lord. Mayhap Emma could be prevailed upon to aid him?'

'Ah, you say that as a jest, my lady, but you have no idea of his powers over women. Pray you never witness it!'

'Will you allow him to visit then?' she asked.

'Pray God, he will join us by winter's end. He was struck down from behind during the battle, but the last word I received said he does yet survive. The duke has also promised Soren lands in the north.'

Giles grew quiet, offering up a prayer in this holy building that Soren did survive and was able to take what was offered them.

Fayth waited for a moment when he grew silent and then asked her questions. 'Do you have other sisters or brothers, Lord Giles?'

'Nay, I was my mother's only child.'

'She yet lives?' she asked.

'Nay,' he replied with a sad smile. 'She is dead these last ten years.'

She knew so little about him and this was her opportunity, for he seemed willing to reveal himself to her now. 'How many years have you?'

'I have twenty-and-three to your ten-and-eight years.'

'So you know my age, then?'

'But, of course, I wanted to know if my bride was long in the tooth or a young woman who still blushed.'

'Ah, but you failed to ask if she was addle-brained as I have been these last few days,' she jested. She watched him approach and stop before her, sitting down in the chair once more.

'Addle-brained? I think not. I have only held these lands for a few sennights and can imagine the pain and anger if I faced losing them. You were born to this and now have lost everyone you held dear and gained only a bastard knight as husband when most certainly your father aimed higher than that for you. Surely I can learn to be lordly and allow you that weakness?'

The sound of Brice shouting outside broke into their silence, alerting them to the demands each one faced. But, Giles hesitated to break their truce and broach the topic he wished to know about most. Still, he must.

'Lady, tell me of Edmund.' Fear filled her gaze then and he shook his head. 'I wish only to know of his claim to you.'

'I do not carry his child, my lord.' The light of recognition lit in her gaze then. 'That is why you wanted to know, because of your own birth?'

'Yes, lady,' he said quietly. 'And I never threatened you or any child you might carry. I simply wanted to know the truth first.'

'There is no child, my lord. He has no claim

on me, other than if we married,' she said with a shake of her head. 'And I suspect that your claim to Taerford is stronger now.'

'He has no claim on your heart, then?' he asked, taking one of her hands in his. Rubbing it gently with his thumb, he was pleased when she did not pull away from his touch.

'Edmund is more brother to me than if he had been one in reality, my lord. There was no attachment like that between us for we each knew our duty.'

'Your father did not betroth you to him before leaving for the north?'

'Nay. Edmund comes from a good Saxon family…and I bethink that his family arranged a marriage for him.' She paused and shook her head again. 'He fostered here, but there were no plans for a betrothal. Until…' Her words drifted off.

'How did he serve your father, lady?' He held his breath, for he suspected that it was not Edmund who served the earl, but…

'As I said, my lord, Edmund fostered here.' She was not going to confirm what he suspected, probably believing that she protected Edmund in some way.

'When did he arrive here in Taerford? How soon after Harold's fall?' That could give him an indication of the possibility of the man's plans and how far he had progressed on them before Giles's arrival.

'Only days before you, my lord, just after I received your missive. He sent out a call to other allies to come and make a stand with him here in Taerford.'

Ah, so Giles's own arrival had put a stop to that gathering, or had it? Reports of bands of rebels came daily from the other Normans in the area. 'And now? Do you know where Edmund and his men are now, lady?'

Fayth shook her head. 'I know not of his condition or whereabouts, my lord. When you had him dragged from the keep, it was the last time I saw him.' There was doubt in her eyes then, as though she did not believe he was alive.

'He left here alive, lady, at your request, and was taken off my lands.' Giles stood then, releasing her hand and walking a few steps away.

'But, if he returns to my lands, I will put him to death.'

She shivered at his words, knowing that he would indeed follow through on that promise. Pray God Edmund had left and sought kith and kin far away from Taerford. Brice knocked on the chapel door and pulled it open before either of them could respond.

'My lord. My lady,' he said with a nod of his head. 'The day is full upon us and there is much to be done. Have you completed your parley or do you need more time to come to arrangements?'

'Brice! Be gone from here. The lady and I are not yet finished,' Giles called out to his friend.

'The sun has broken through the clouds, my lord. Make haste for there is much to be done.' The other knight closed the door and called out to someone else in the yard, his voice carrying through the closed door.

'My lord, I should go,' she said, standing before him.

'Wait but for one more moment, lady.'

Fayth faced him now. There was something

more to be said between them. He gambled by taking her hands in his as he spoke.

'On the matter of your father's death, I know only that I served Duke William from my place in his left flank, where all the Bretons fought under the command of my uncle, Alain Fergant of Brittany. There is no way to know where your father fought or if we engaged each other during the battles that day.'

He tugged her closer, letting go of her hands to reach up and shift the drooping circlet that held her veil in place. She'd not even realised it had fallen to one side until he righted it.

'If you would hate me, hate me for things I do and not for those I cannot answer for.'

She did not meet his gaze then; instead she stared at the proof of her father's death, dangling there around his neck, in view of one and all.

Her father's ring.

'But you have his ring, my lord,' she said, and if her tone was harsh, it was due to the pain that seized her heart whenever she saw it there. 'He would never willingly give that up while alive.'

He shook his head. 'The duke's man presented

this to me when he gave me the grant of lands and the betrothal contract. I did not remove this from your father's hand.'

'Truly?'

Such terrible images of this knight killing her father and taking the ring from him had plagued her since she'd seen it on the chain around his neck. Those thoughts had plagued her even more so in the aftermath of the pleasure she had received at his hands.

He took her hands in his then and lifted them before her. Kissing each one, he met her gaze. 'But do not be fooled into believing I may not have been the one who cut him down. I know I ended many lives on the battlefield that day. I cannot know who died by my hands.'

Brice called again outside and she watched a smile fill Giles's face now. 'You see how exasperating he can be, my lord?' she said.

He yet held her hands as he lowered them, but kept one in his grasp. Bringing it back to his mouth, he turned it and placed his mouth on her wrist. The heat from his mouth made her blood race and she could feel the pulse of it under his lips.

'I do not ask you to forget our differences, lady, but only to allow time for us to become accustomed to each other before laying judgement on me.'

A strange request coming from the man who had fought his way here, allowing no one to stop him from taking her and her lands. And from one carrying the orders of his duke and the rights to all he claimed in service to his lord. And from a man who had the power and the strength to take whatever, and whomever, he wanted with no one to stop him.

Yet, he asked.

'Very well,' she whispered.

'Brice is anxious to get to work. Come, I will take you to the village so you may begin your work there.'

'Verily, my lord?' Stunned as he acquiesced to her earlier request, she wondered what had caused him to change his mind.

'You may only go there with my express permission and never without Brice or Roger with you. Do you understand my words on this?'

'Yes, my lord.'

Her heart lightened at the thought of leaving

the keep for even a short time, to see how the surrounding lands had fared after the attacks, and how the rest of the villagers were coping, as well as tending to the needs of those who lived outside the walls.

Fayth watched as Giles pulled open the door of the chapel and followed him outside where, indeed, the sun did shine as Brice had reported. The Breton stopped to speak with his friend, who continued to look round at her. Did he think she'd been harmed in some way?

As she gazed around, many of those working in the yard stopped and watched her, too. Even Father Henry, who stood near the well speaking to the boy Durwyn, stared openly. It was obvious that the exchange between them in the hall and her escape to the chapel had drawn some untoward attention. Excusing herself from Giles with a word, she made her way to the priest.

'How do you fare, Lady Fayth?' he asked, searching her face intently as though the answer could be seen there. 'Was I mistaken in placing some trust in this new lord's word?'

'I think some things are settled between us,

Father,' she said, nodding at him, yet looking back at the man under discussion.

Who stood looking at her.

Heat pulsed then through her as he stared at her, his thoughts clear in his gaze. Her body ached to feel his touch then, indeed, it remembered the pleasure wrought by his hands on her skin. Shivering even in the sun's warmth, she shook herself free of such thoughts and listened to Father Henry's counsel.

'Marriage is not easy in the best of times, but it is your duty now to cleave to your husband and accept his rule. Even your father would have counselled you so.'

'Even if he is the enemy?' How could that be reconciled with faith or conscience?

Taking her hand and drawing her close, he answered in a soft voice. 'Many of these Norman invaders are not honouring their pledge to accept the daughters of fallen lords to wife. I have heard tales of Saxon women being used—' he paused as though searching for the correct word '—harshly and then being put off their own lands.'

He patted her hand and smiled. 'This lord

looks as if he knows both the good and bad life has to offer and appears to be seeking the better way here. It is not wrong to help him along that path, child, or to accept his efforts in good stead.'

Father Henry's words gave her hope. She could not and would not forget her husband's part in the battle between their peoples and their lords, but it was not sinful to allow him to prove himself to them.

'Lady?'

She turned when Giles called her. 'I will take you to the village now for a short visit. Come, gather what you need from the keep and we will go.'

'You see? He listens and considers your words before he acts.' Father Henry released her hand. 'Go now, child. Seek your lord.'

Fayth went off to the keep to get her cloak and her parchments on which she was keeping records of their stores.

Chapter Eleven

'Did you swive her on the floor of God's House?' Brice asked under his breath as the lady walked by them on her way into the keep. Giles speared him a look that bespoke of the falseness of such a thought, but Brice shrugged. 'You were in there a long time, Giles.'

'In spite of what Soren might tell you, some things are not accomplished quickly, my friend. As you will discover in Thaxted, I am certain.'

'Mayhap I will walk in and be lauded as the conquering hero? What say you then?'

'I will add that to my nightly prayers to the Almighty, Brice.' They laughed at his words and then Giles sobered. ''Tis like a boil was lanced—so much had built between us and needed to be released.'

'A good tupping would accomplish the same

release, my lord.' Brice laughed and added, 'Or so Soren would say.'

'I pray it will be so, my lord Thaxted. Soon and often.'

They walked the rest of the way to the stables and mounted the horses waiting saddled for them. Ordering four others to await them at the gates, Giles waited on the lady. Glancing down at the ring he wore on a chain around his neck, he lifted it for closer inspection. Bertram's ring bore a large red stone carved with his insignia—a raven and a river—and nothing else. Except, he noticed, a large dent-like indentation on the rim of it, cracking the edge of the stone, as though it had been hit with something. Was that how it had been removed from the old lord's finger? No wonder Fayth became overwrought whenever she saw it.

She came through the door then and he rode over to her, leaning down and holding out a hand to help her mount. Her confusion was clear.

'You will not walk into the village,' he said, holding his hand out again. ''Tis not safe.'

She gathered her skirts, accepted his hand

and, with a foot placed on his, climbed up behind him on the horse. Once she'd settled there and he felt her arms encircle him, he signalled to ride out. As they made their way out of the gates and down the road to the village by the river his heated body reacted to her nearness and soon the ride was more uncomfortable than he'd have wished it to be. They rode along the narrow path and it did not take long before he could feel her fidgeting behind him.

'Hold there, my lady. Have you never ridden before?' he asked.

'You are too tall, my lord. I can see nothing past your shoulders as we ride.' He thought that made perfect protective sense, but the lady seemed more interested in the sights they were passing.

'Lady, I am not convinced that you are safe leaving the manor's walls. Do not give me reasons to return there now.'

Brice smiled wryly at him, obviously enjoying the situation. No matter his friend's reassurances that no rebels remained on his lands, Giles could not pretend to be comforted by such reports. If his suspicions were correct about

Edmund, then they were close by. She did settle behind him then and he enjoyed the feel of her arms wrapped around his waist and her body pressed close to his. They made their way to the edge of the village where more of his men waited.

When his men spread out down the main village path to the edge of the clearing and gave a signal, he let Brice assist the lady down. He had no intention of dismounting, for he could respond to an attack faster and more efficiently on horseback than on foot. Bow and sword at the ready, he turned and positioned himself where he could see the most.

Giles sat watching as Fayth walked down the path and was greeted by more and more of the villagers there. As her presence became known those not working away from the centre of the village all came to see her. Brice, with a nod from him, proceeded ahead and checked some of the storage buildings there while Fayth continued talking. When about an hour had passed and the skies began to grow dark with a coming storm, Giles called an end to it and summoned both the lady and Brice.

Although at first she seemed to be ready to protest, she bade the people a farewell and gave a promise to return. Then she walked to him. She did not hesitate as she approached Giles and somehow that made his heart glad. She looked not with dread as she held her hand out first for his and when he helped her up behind him she seemed to be at peace with him and his orders.

'A storm is coming, lady. You will have more time on the morrow to see your people.'

'You will allow this?' she asked.

'I would rather if you did not, but with Brice or Roger at your side I will permit such visits.'

She said nothing in reply, but if he was made to, Giles would have sworn an oath that her arms tightened at that moment. When she rested her head against his back, he could not help the smile that broke on his face.

The rest of their journey was silent. He stopped just inside the gates at her request to let her dismount and then rode the horse to the stables. By the time he returned to the hall to discuss his coming journey with her, she was gone. Asking the servants about her led him to the chamber that had been hers. He pushed open the door, unsure of what he'd find.

Edmund advanced as close as he could to the village without being seen. He'd left most of his men at the fork in the river and returned to see what the messenger had reported. Now, not only were the villagers back with tales of the new lord's words and pledges to protect them, but, worse, they believed him!

His strategy to gain control of Taerford and hold this area of his father's lands had failed so far—the arrival and success of this Breton knight had put a halt to his control so far. But with help from the other displaced Saxon lords, he planned to wrest this important estate from its invader lord and use it as his base to reclaim the lands that should be his.

Not all Saxons had been thrown off their lands. Those who submitted to William retained theirs, but submitting did not ensure a lord's loyalties. And with the backing of the Northumbrian earls, though once his father's enemies, he would remove the Norman blight on their lands.

Forced to creep like a thief behind and between cottages and sheds to remain unseen, he was able to get close enough to see Fayth. She looked well, pale, but unharmed as much as he could tell. The lord brought her to the village himself and sat watching as she spoke to the villagers. The other one, the one called Brice, made his way along the path, looking in cottages as he went. It was a near thing several times, but Edmund was practised now and could move about without being seen.

After some time had passed, the knight called out to Fayth and she went to him without delay. Narrowing his eyes, he watched as they exchanged words and she said farewell to the villagers with a promise to return. And then, without a moment's hesitation, Fayth gave her hand to the Breton and climbed up behind him!

He could forgive her much for her willingness to place her life in danger for his and to plead for him, which had resulted in his freedom and his chance to regroup and challenge again. Surely, she did what she must to survive and if it meant submission to this Breton puppet of the Norman duke, he would understand. Stepping back into the shadows, he swore an oath on his father's soul that, no matter what it took to free her, she would not suffer this Breton's control of her for long.

Leaving three men to keep watch over the village from the other side of the river, Edmund travelled back to his camp, hoping that others brought back news better than his.

Fayth sat on the floor before the large wooden chest, searching through it for the smaller casket where she kept her personal things. She had feared looking for it before this, for, by rights, it all belonged to her new husband. Surely, though, he would not begrudge her a few small trifles to remind her of her parents. Leaning against the chest, she opened the box that had been a present to her on the twelfth anniversary of her birth. The intricate carving and decorations were still beautiful and reminded her of the care that had gone into making the box.

Edmund had claimed to be inexperienced at woodworking, but the results proved him wrong. To this day, he would carve a piece of wood into small shapes when he needed time to examine his thoughts—or he had, before this war had come to their gates.

Moving the top items aside, Fayth reached to the bottom and took out the two rings there. Not big enough to draw attention, they both still carried memories of her parents. A matching pair, one larger for a man's finger and one smaller for a woman's, these were the rings her parents had exchanged at their betrothal ceremony. Her father's liege lord had gifted them with the rings as a sign of his support for the coming marriage of Bertram, heir to Taerford, to Willa, a distant cousin of Earl Harold.

Searching in the box, she found the scrap of ribbon and tied them back together so as not to lose one or the other. Just as she was about to return the box to its place in the bottom of her chest she realised she was not alone. Looking up, she met her husband's gaze.

'What is that?' he asked, coming towards her and crouching down. She handed him the box and watched as he examined it. 'The workmanship is excellent. Is this yours?'

'Aye, my lord. A gift from a…cousin,' she

replied, not wanting to mention and explain Edmund's true place in her or her father's life.

'And inside?' he asked, handing the box back to her.

She opened it and showed him the ribbons and circlets for her veils and then decided to show him the rings. As she held them out he frowned at them.

'I know that they are yours by right, my lord, but they are all I have left of my parents and would beg—'

'Do not beg, Fayth.' He placed the rings in her hand. 'These are yours and I would not take them.' He closed her fingers over the rings and stepped away. 'If I had wanted them, I would have taken them when my men found them.'

'You knew of them? How?' she asked.

'My men searched everything in the keep, every room, every chest or trunk, every nook or hidey hole where something of value could be hidden. 'Tis the way,' he said with a shrug. He turned as though to leave and then faced her again. 'But what made you seek them out today?'

'I have thought of little else this day, but

my parents. When you stood in the hall and announced yourself lord here, accepting the pledges of those in service to you, and when you faced me so forthrightly and tried to make me understand about my father's death and your part—' he raised his brows at that, so she continued '—or not in it, or then the way you gave me orders about the village, all of those things reminded me of the way my father and mother ruled here.' She climbed to her feet and held the rings out to him once more.

'I would like you to keep these as a sign of my pledge this day to you.'

She'd surprised him, she knew it, for his mouth opened and closed several times before he actually spoke. 'Nay, lady. I have no need of your parents' rings.' Fayth watched as he took the rings from her, placed them back in the box and handed it to her, looking on as she placed it back at the bottom of the chest.

'I would ask for your honest efforts rather than a grand showing like this. And, though I am not questioning your intentions, I think you do this from all of the emotions of this day and not in the same way that those in the hall pledged to me this morn.'

'But you demanded it of them, and you accepted their gestures,' she argued. 'Do you not expect the same of me?'

'What I want from you is different, lady. I want more than just your labours or words. I want you, heart, body and soul.'

Overwhelmed by his words and what they meant, she shivered. 'But you do not want me. You said you will not…' Now when she needed to say it, the words escaped her.

'Bed you?' he offered.

Fayth shook her head, no longer trusting words.

Lord Giles stepped closer and took her hand once more. Pulling her towards him, he lifted his hauberk and placed her hand against his body. That part of him sprang to life, hardening as he held her hand there.

'Oh, make no mistake, lady. I want you.' He released her hand and she drew it back, feeling out of breath from the contact and what she knew it meant. 'If I could believe your words, I would take you into our chambers, strip you naked and not stop until we exhaust ourselves in bedplay.'

Before, she might not have understood, but after last evening's pleasuring she could only imagine what that meant. Her body grew hot and wet in the places he'd touched as she waited for his words…or touch. He dropped the shirt of metal from his grasp and took a breath then.

'Wanting you is not as important to me as knowing the truth and so I wait. But know this, I am tempted today to believe your words. I want to believe them. It is just not in me to do that now.'

If he'd said those words a day ago, they would have infuriated her. Now, after his disclosures today in the chapel, she understood a bit better his need for proof. Though it still stung her that he could not—or would not—believe her. Bastards were part of life and many in their culture inherited alongside their legitimate siblings, but she knew that was not generally true in Norman or Breton life. And in spite of Giles's duke being one, it was still not accepted by most in high standing.

'Very well,' she said, trying to understand and

yet not. 'Were you looking for me, my lord, when you came in?' She brushed her hands over her tunic to smooth it.

'Ah, yes,' he said, smiling at her. His eyes seemed more blue now and his face appeared much younger when he smiled, not so fearsome as it did when he raged in anger.

'I decided to wait until the morrow before leaving to see the extent of the lands. So I thought that you and Brice could share the noon meal with me and we can make plans about moving whatever supplies are left in the village to the keep on my return?'

'Very well, my lord. Mayhap someday you will reveal to me what places Brice so far in your debt that he will follow me around with little argument?'

He held out his hand to her and she placed hers there. As he guided her out of her former chamber she walked at his side knowing there must be much, much more that he was not going to say about his friend.

'What makes you think it is with little arguing? Mayhap I have saved your tender sensibilities from having to listen to it?'

They reached the main floor and the object of their discussions stood waiting for them. They shared a glance between them and when he glared at both of them, they laughed. Brice joined them at table as they made plans for the rest of the day, as well as the three more that Lord Giles would be away.

It was during that meal that Fayth discovered another of her husband's secrets—one he and Brice shared and both tried to hide. So obvious to her now, she wondered how she had missed it before. And wondered whether or not to reveal her knowledge of it to him.

Neither her husband nor his friend could read.

Though not a terrible lack, for many noble Saxons could not read or write, to them it was surely another mark of their illegitimacy and another quality found lacking.

Fayth stored away that bit of knowledge, not certain where or when it would be of the most use to her.

Chapter Twelve

The door opened quietly as it always did when her husband tried to enter their chambers softly. Fayth sat in the tall chair, with only a few candles lit, a blanket wrapped around her shoulders, offering up her nightly prayers and waiting for him. Giles nodded as she untangled the string of prayer beads from her hands and put them in the sack on the table.

'When do you leave, my lord?'

'At first light.' He faced her and placed his hands on his hips, with a stern expression in his eyes. 'While we are in our chambers, could you use my given name?'

She thought she might have screamed it out when he'd pleasured her and her face grew hot as she remembered.

'*My lords* are for others, lady,' he said. 'In return, I shall remember to call you Fayth.'

'Are you not yet accustomed to your rank and its privileges?' she asked. 'Or do you think of someone else when you hear it?'

'Very astute, lady.' He nodded. 'I am not accustomed and I do think of someone else when I hear it. My father's father was called Giles, so I expect to see him enter whenever I hear "Lord Giles" said.' He grew solemn then. 'And since he did not wish to lay eyes on me, it was never a good thing when he did.'

He began undressing and she tried not to watch, but after she had seen him work in the yard in only his breeches and after she had felt him against her last night, his body did interest her. Even knowing it was unseemly for a well-born lady to be curious about such things, she could not stop watching him now.

Giles paused in undressing, mostly because the sound of his wife's shallow breathing as she watched him was arousing him. If truth be told, everything she did or said aroused him. His plan of exhausting himself before climbing into bed with her had not worked, so he thought he would try coming to bed awake enough to control his wayward desire. As he noticed her eyes staring at his cock as it extended itself and hardened in his breeches he knew that would not work either.

Thinking of other things, or attempting to, he realised that he had not had a woman since before leaving Normandy. That was most definitely part of the problem, for when he spoke of the heat of battle, he meant it. The rage and excitement of facing one's foes and fighting for your life, or theirs, created a powerful rush of blood and made most men hard. And that led to the rape and pillaging by those men who could not be controlled.

The biggest part of his problem, though, was the woman who continued to gaze at his manhood and who would share the bed with him that night.

'Mayhap you should get into bed now, lady?'

'Your pardon, my…' She paused as he narrowed his eyes at her and shook his head. 'Giles,' she whispered instead. 'I was distracted.'

She said it with no attempt to be humorous, for he suspected she was as innocent of the events between men and women as she seemed to be, and yet she kept looking at him and not moving from the chair.

He walked past her and nearly tore the coverings from the bed in his attempts to lift them and hasten her entrance into it. Finally, she dropped the blanket from her shoulders and, lifting her shift, climbed up on the bed and over to the far side. He decided to be blunt with her, or the night would be a long, sleepless one for him.

'Are you reticent about what happens between us because I am not of your rank?' He could not say the word to her; it carried such shame for him. She turned on her side and watched as he put out the candles and approached the bed.

'Not of my rank?' she asked and he could see the hint of a smile on her lips. 'Truly, I think the problem lies not with the status of your birth but with the place of it and how you came to be here.' She brushed her hair over her shoulder with her hand and watched him closely. 'Even our King Harold had two wives at the same time and children by both. They cannot all be legitimate, can they?'

Stunned by her admission and her logic, he laughed. 'One would think not.'

He untied his breeches and tugged them down, over his erect manhood. He tossed them on the chair and then went through his routine of placing his sword and dagger within an arm's length. Giles turned and put out the last candle in full view of her before following her under the coverings. This time, for the first time, he left no layers between them.

Giles settled beside her and pondered his next move. Still of a mind to ease her into love-making by introducing her a step at a time, so that she was ready once he had his answer, he thought to use her curiosity. First, though, he must make certain of one thing.

'I would pleasure you, lady, but fear it causing you distress.' She gasped then. Mayhap a bit too blunt? 'I thought you enjoyed it last night, but then your tears confused me and I would not touch you if it pains you.'

'I hesitate to speak on such things, but my father always said I spoke too much like a man, my lord. He said it was ever my failing.' She let out a loud sigh and then he felt her turn towards him in the bed. 'I liked what happened between us, but I feel as though I am being faithless to my family and my people if I seek your touch.'

'I am your husband, before God and your people. I have the right to…'

Her finger laid across his lips shocked him. 'You have been patient with my hesitation, Giles, when another man…'

'Another Norman?' he offered.

'Another conqueror,' she corrected, 'would not be so.'

She was so close to allowing him and he did not wish to jeopardise her taking the step on her own, but his body burned for her. 'There is another way,' he suggested, not daring to think it could work.

Before she could say another word, he turned her onto her back and covered her with his body. Taking her hands in his and stretching them over her head, he kissed her, pressing his lips against hers until she opened for him. He traced the outline of her lips with his tongue before taking her mouth with his. He swept his tongue into her mouth, seeking her, and then suckled on it when she touched it to his.

Then he stopped.

Lifting his face from hers, he whispered, 'Some men would force it on you, force you to accept their touch.'

He now caught both hands in one and used the other to trace along her arm to her side and then up onto her breast. Her nipple pebbled against his palm. Her body reacted to his touch and he felt as though he had lost his mind. Leaning down, he possessed her mouth with his until they both lost their breaths.

'Some like the use of force,' he said to test her reaction. 'They like to be held against their will and made to accept all manner of pleasures forced on them.' He reached down and tugged her shift up until it reached her waist.

'Nay! Truly?' she asked then in a breathy voice.

Giles leaned over and kissed the nipple of her breast even through the linen that covered it, licking at it and using his teeth against it before sucking it into his mouth and possessing that, too.

Instead of raging, she seemed to melt against him and writhed under his body. Trying to remember the point he was making, he eased off to one side and slid his leg up between hers until it pressed at the junction of her thighs. She gasped but did not protest and when he felt the wetness between her legs on his, he slid it further between, enjoying the slickness her body wept on him.

'Truly,' he whispered. 'A woman who is overpowered has no choice—she cannot be blamed for what happens.'

Still holding her hands above her head, he moved to the other breast and teased it as he had the first. While sucking on the hardened tip of that one, he opened his hand wide on her bare skin under her shift and slid it down over her ribs, then over her stomach towards the place where his leg lay holding her in place.

'Nay,' she cried out, stopping his every movement.

'Hush,' he said, leaning against her cheek, 'it is all in jest, lady.' He released her hands and whispered, 'I would never take you in force, lady, nor anger.'

Though his body screamed in rage at him for stopping. His cock wanted nothing so much as to bury itself hilt deep in her heat and wetness. His blood pounded through his veins, demanding that he take her and take her hard and deep. Giles rolled off her knowing he must catch hold of his lust before he did what he'd promised her he would not.

'Have I frightened you beyond words now, lady?'

'I did not want you to believe you had to force me to this, Giles,' she said softly. 'I took a vow and am your wife. If you seek pleasure in our marriage bed, I will not refuse you.'

'Not refuse me? Will you lie there like something dead and allow my touch, lady? I think that would be worse than not touching you at all.'

Would he for ever be the bastard child begging for something from his betters? He knew that a woman of Fayth's rank and breeding did not consort with bastard and landless knights, unless she was seeking some amusement or attention when her lord husband was being pleasured by his leman or whore.

'I do not think I could lie motionless if you touch me the way you just did.'

He turned on his side towards her now. 'I had thought to ease your way into relations with me, instead of waiting until you have your courses and then taking you. I had thought we could become accustomed in this manner.' He tried to explain and would have but she stopped him once more with her finger across his lips.

'Then accustom me to your touch, husband,' she whispered.

He kissed her fingers and took her hand in his. 'Will you cry after I do?'

Silence answered him instead of words. Then she moved closer to him on the bed. 'I cannot promise that I will not cry, Giles, but I will try not to let it happen.'

He considered letting go of this mad plan until he felt her hand slide down onto his chest and into the hair there. He rolled onto his back and let her explore him as she pleased. Until, that was, she reached his cock and tried to touch him there. Giles stayed her hand. 'Nay, not that.'

'Does it hurt, then? To touch it?' she asked.

'In a way I cannot explain, lady, but I can show you.'

He released her hand and moved his to her

legs, caressing them until they trembled beneath his fingers. Giles reached over and lifted her leg over his hip, drawing her closer and opening her to his exploration. Gliding over the curls and then her stomach and then back, he listened as her breathing came faster and faster. Using his fingers and his thumb, he spread the folds of her womanhood apart and pressed against the hardened bud there.

'Does it hurt to touch there?' he asked.

She arched into his hand even more and keened out a throaty moan as she did it. The passionate noises continued as he brought her to the edge of release time and time again, but would not let her over it. When she could only moan in wordless sounds, he pressed his palm against her curls and his finger against that sensitive place until he felt her spasm against his hand. Holding her tightly there, he waited as her release rolled over her and until she fell onto her back, her leg grazing his hardness as she did.

Giles was tempted to seek his own release until she reached over and touched him there. 'Nay, lady, do not,' he began.

'Did you not say you would call me Fayth,

Giles?' she asked as she began to slide her hand down his rod. 'Help me,' she whispered. 'I know not how…'

'Fayth,' he said on a groan as her innocent caress proved more stirring than a practised one could.

He captured her hands and guided her movements until it was his turn to moan out his release. He felt her lay back and, trying to rearrange the bedclothes, he discovered that she had already fallen asleep. Making certain she was covered, he turned on his side.

His last thought as sleep took him was that if there was this pleasure without being inside her, what could it be like when he was planted deep within?

He was gone in the morning when she woke and it was only when Ardith tended to the fire that she discovered that he'd given orders for her to be left undisturbed. Since the chamber was dark and only the occasional sound of thunder rumbled overhead, she knew that going to the village was not a possibility this day. Accepting his gift of staying in bed long past daybreak, Fayth fell back into the arms of sleep.

It was some time later that day when her courses started. As two days passed and the third began she wondered what his reaction would be to the news that she was the virgin she swore herself to be.

The bad storms continued for those three days, unabated, and she thought he must be wholly uncomfortable surveying his lands in the relentless rain. They had spoken of her father's lands, now his, but she was unfamiliar with the neighbouring ones. She knew one reason he rode was that he sought a location on which to build a new keep in the Norman fashion.

Fayth had been working in the small room off the hall where she kept all the records of the manor, as her father had before her, when she had happened to overhear Giles speaking to his friend about the need of a defensible keep.

As much as she'd like to believe that fighting was over, she feared it was not. Each day brought reports of sightings of outlaws and William's move north- and westward. Brice accepted them on Giles's behalf from the messengers sent by their Norman neighbours or from the king. And the knight was none too happy when news of his own holding did not arrive.

When nothing could be moved because the wagons became mired in the muddy roads and the rain and winds continued into that third day, Brice sought relief the way men did—he challenged several of the other knights to swordplay. The rains kept her inside and no amount of cajoling would make her venture forth to see him defeat his opponents.

Finally, the fourth morning after Giles left, the sun rose full in the sky, blessing the cold, wet ground with warmth and light. The roads began to dry out late in the morning and Fayth decided it was time to venture back into the village and try to complete some of the work she'd set out to do before her husband's return.

Chapter Thirteen

Fayth finished the last part of her inventory in the weaver's hut and wrote down the information on her parchment scroll before she forgot. Brice appeared at the door.

'Lady, sundown is approaching. How much longer will you need before you are ready to return to the keep?' he asked.

Looking around the hut, she noticed one more pile of bolts of material that she'd missed. They were lucky this cottage did not burn during the attack, for they would have lost a fortune in a goodly amount of woven fabrics her father had purchased at market just this past summer.

'Not much longer, sir. A short while?' she asked.

'Then heed my call this time and do not make me come searching for you,' he said, brusquely.

He paused and gave her an apologetic glance. 'My lady.' He bowed before leaving the cottage.

She'd been the bane of his existence these last days and he served as an example to her of why a man-of-war needed to be a man-at-war. She had no idea why his duke delayed in granting Brice the lands promised, but he did not handle the waiting well. Fayth smiled to herself over the many examples of his impatience she'd seen since Giles had left the keep, and she would not be surprised if there was a fight when he returned.

Would it be today? He was at least a day late, but he had sent word back late yesterday that he needed another day. Yet, sundown approached with no sign of him on the roads leading through the village or to the manor. A tightness in the pit of her stomach grew at the thought of his return. An unnatural, she was certain, anticipation of completing the marital act with him left her breathless at times, and she imagined—or tried to—what wondrous things he would show her and do to her now that she could prove her honour was intact.

She forced herself to breathe slowly and to

push such thoughts of lust and passion from her mind, especially when she had work to complete. Her body fought her efforts, tingling and throbbing in those private places where he had pleasured her with his hands and his mouth. What would it feel like when he finally joined to her with that part of him that she'd caressed so intimately? Would the thickness and length of him hurt as he took her maidenhead and made her his wife in reality?

Her mouth grew dry, but that place between her legs where he would thrust and complete the marriage act grew wetter and wetter with each wicked thought. Dabbing at her heated face with the edge of her sleeve, she turned her attentions back to the work before her.

Fayth had divided the final pile of fabrics by type and was measuring and counting as fast as she could when the cottage door opened once more.

'Your pardon, Sir Brice. I did not hear your call,' she began, turning to face his bluster. But it was not Brice who stood before her.

Edmund Haroldson, the man who should be Earl of Wessex and heir to the throne of

England, ducked into the cottage and quickly pulled the door closed behind him. So shocked was she that Fayth could only blink and gape at him.

'Fayth!' he whispered to her. 'Are you well?'

He held his arms open to her and she ran into his embrace. His arms, strong and tight around her, comforted her as none others had since her father's departure to the north. She clutched him just as fiercely as the memories of her life before the duke's arrival on their shores passed through her mind. Only when he leaned away did she loosen her hold on him.

'Edmund! You should not be here,' she warned. 'Lord Giles's men are positioned throughout the village. You cannot let them capture you.'

She ran to the small shuttered window and opened it only enough to permit herself a view down the main path of the village. She could see Brice off in the distance. Turning back to her father's liege lord, she shook her head and ran to his side. Claiming another embrace, she waited for him to speak.

'They will not capture me, Fayth. Fear not. I

still have many who aid me, both here and in the keep.'

'Spies?' she asked, even as her stomach churned at the thought. He nodded in answer. 'Why are you here?'

'I am here for you, Fayth. You did not think I would abandon you to these Norman pigs after you risked your life for me?' He drew her to him and kissed her on the forehead. 'Your words and actions saved many lives that day and I only pray you have not been mistreated because of it. King Edgar was impressed when I told him of your courage.'

Fayth began to answer, but Edmund waved her off. 'I have only a few moments but want to tell you I understand that he has forced you into marriage.' The bile rose in her stomach now as he spoke of her husband. 'You do what you must to survive, Fayth. Submit to him until I can free you from this unholy joining. Our good Saxon lords and their men are rising up—'

'Edmund, you must listen to me,' she interrupted. 'This lord is not unkind to me. He has forced nothing on me to which I did not give consent. You should leave this area, leave Wessex, before it is too late.'

He stared at her as though a stranger now. Holding her by the shoulders and searching her face, he shook his head.

'Tell me you have not fallen for his kind words and lies, Fayth? Swear to me that you will avenge your father's death at his hands.'

She stumbled then, not accepting his words. 'It was a battle with thousands of men, Edmund. The chances that he was the one are...' Cool logic had led her to that conclusion in the dark of the night as she considered Lord Giles's explanation.

'There were witnesses, Fayth,' he said solemnly. 'Some of your father's men survived and now fight at my side.'

She heard the words, but she'd convinced herself that Giles had played no part in killing her father. Now, she feared that she had been lulled for his own purposes and hers.

'This lord who treats you well is no different from the one who took the rest of Leofwyne's lands. That one has branded the people, like the lowest of cattle, and cuts off a foot or hand if they are caught trying to escape.'

She gasped at the horror, shaking her head in denial.

'These Normans follow their master well, Fayth. They yet practise the atrocities they brought with them, learned from the ruthlessness of William the Bastard.' He shook her shoulders and forced her to meet his gaze. 'How long until this lord begins to show his true nature? When there is not enough grain to get through the winter do you think it will be his Norman and Breton knights who starve or your people? Our people?'

A whistling caught his attention and he released her. 'His man comes now. You must go to him, but hold strong, Fayth. I am putting my plans in place and will send for you when I can. Watch for a message.'

Shaking and confused by his claims, she accepted his quick kiss and watched as he hid in one of the alcoves of the cottage. Just as she was about to open the door, he whispered yet again.

'I will bring you proof of your father's death at his hands so that you can rest easy when we dispatch the bastard who thinks himself high enough to claim Taerford, and you.'

Fayth lifted the latch on the door and opened it, leaving the cottage and walking onto the path so that Brice would see her and stop his approach. Edmund would probably wait until dark to make his way out of the hut and back to wherever he hid. When Brice went straight for the door, and stood searching around the hut with his sharp gaze, Fayth knew he was suspicious.

'Is aught wrong, my lady?' he looked back at her and asked.

Sickened by Edmund's words, she took a deep breath, but found it worsened the roiling of her stomach. Worse, her legs trembled and her head began to spin with dizziness.

'I am not well...'

He caught her just as her legs buckled and held her as her stomach rebelled against all she'd heard. She remembered little else until she woke in her bed in the keep with Emma at her side.

Giles entered the keep and found it as silent as a church. His men sat at table, Brice in his chair, but no one spoke or argued as usually happened. Tired, hungry and angry, he wanted a good meal, a cup of wine and his bed.

He wanted his wife, too, but that did not seem to change and she was not present in the hall. He'd been hard for days now and every memory of her skin, her touch on him, her taste, made it worse. Now, he needed to speak to Brice and his commanders before he could seek her out. The grave expressions on the faces of his men spoke of other matters. Brice stood at his approach and drew him off to the side for a private word.

'The lady fell ill,' Brice began. 'It started while we were in the village today and she is abed now.'

Giles started in the direction of the stairs even before he decided to go to her. 'Is it the fever?'

He moved quickly, taking the steps two at a time to reach their chambers faster, not waiting for an answer. The old woman Emma sat before their door and she stood as he came closer. Truly he caught but a few words of her explanation—bleeding, courses, stomach, posset, sleeping—but he did gather that she did not seem in danger.

With a word to Emma to stay, he opened the door and walked to the bed. He had to search in the low light of the few lit candles to find her, so swallowed up amongst the coverings and the pillows was she. Not knowing why the thought of her ill bothered him so, he reached out and touched her cheek. He offered up a brief prayer of thanks that it felt cool to his touch.

Before he could wake her, he stepped away from the bed and left the chamber. With Emma remaining to oversee the lady's care, and Brice trailing his steps, he went back to the hall where he found the meal and wine he'd wanted. But as he shared the news of the surrounding area with his men he found his appetite had deserted him.

William had given the lands adjoining his to Huard de Vassey, one of the duke's most ruthless men, but one who had supported William from the start in his campaign to control England. Giles had seen the man in battle, and as lord of his lands, and knew that no one enjoyed the suffering and misery of others more. Pray God, Lord Huard would return to Normandy and his seneschal would be more tolerant of the Saxons under his rule.

Pray God!

From what Giles had heard, Huard was beginning as he meant to go on and had already undertaken the complete subjugation of anyone or anything Saxon on his property. Giles suspected that his lands would be the first place anyone running from Huard's harsh rule would come.

And they must be prepared, for under law a lord had the right to seek and gain back runaway serfs. He could punish them as he saw fit, though leaving them alive enough to work was always a consideration. Since many of those granted lands already held land and titles on the continent, they could call for more labourers and knights from home to help them in England.

Until England was settled and William's rule uncontested, the Norman lords would be best advised to tread carefully, as William's man had informed him when he had received his grant. Take the lands, secure the lands, control the people, get heirs and keep the lands. Simple, clear instructions on William's wishes for his new English subjects, but each lord would decide his manner and methods themselves, leading to many variations, hence the difference between Giles's way and Huard's.

Giles emptied two cups of wine before he felt ready to discuss this subject with Brice, for his friend would no doubt face similar challenges. After completing the report to his commanders and hearing theirs, he dismissed them and continued talking to Brice late into the night about his plans to aid any of those who escaped Huard's cruelty.

Though it was a dangerous endeavor, neither he nor Brice could allow such brutality to go unanswered and unopposed. If his opposition and actions must be done quietly and with little or no notice, so be it. Lord Gautier's lessons sank deep into his soul and he would keep his honour by carrying out clandestine rescues of those unfortunates trapped in Huard's power.

It was not until later, as he climbed the stairs to his chambers, that Emma's words finally struck him—the lady's courses were upon her.

The realisation froze him there as he thought on all that meant to him, to her and to their future.

Fayth did not carry Edmund's child.

Their link was severed and their paths went in different directions. Anything that had happened between them in the past was simply that—past.

Giles was her future and she would, God willing, bear his children to carry his name. As he waved Emma off to her own pallet and lifted the latch on the door he almost laughed. He knew it would not be as easy as that, but he suspected that once she was with child he could claim her fierce loyalties. Pushing the door open, he moved quietly as he took off his clothing, placed his sword down and climbed into the bed. Or tried to, for the lady now lay sleeping in the very centre.

Easing her onto her side, he slid down next to her. She stirred, but he whispered to her, urging her back to sleep, for Emma had revealed how much work she'd accomplished before taking ill. Her gentle breathing told him she had succumbed, but in her sleep she leaned back against his body and rested there.

After four days on the road, riding and sleeping in the torrential rains, with the cold seeping into his bones, nothing could have felt better than this. Her soft bottom against his groin did not inflame him this once; instead he held her close and breathed in her scent, finding comfort there. The horrors he'd seen and learned of, and his worries for their future, faded away as he lay there with her. Although he thought he would not gain sleep this night, he felt it tugging him down.

In that moment, nothing could feel more right to him.

When he woke and saw the fear back in her eyes, he wondered when things had gone awry.

Chapter Fourteen

Giles woke to find Fayth sitting against the wall staring at him. Her face was pale, but it was the fear in her gaze that drew his attention. Pushing his hair out of his eyes, he leaned up on his elbows and tried to figure out what had happened.

'I need to use the chamber pot, my lord,' she said.

Well, that would be one thing he had not considered. He usually left the room as soon as he rose, leaving her to her ablutions in private. This was the first morning since sharing a bed that he had not.

'You should have woken me,' he replied as the other reason she needed privacy occurred to him.

Her courses were still upon her.

Grabbing up his clothes and weapons, he opened the door and called for Emma. 'She will see to your needs, Fayth.'

These female bodily functions were a mystery to him and one he would rather avoid. Though most women he knew dealt with it matter-of-factly, they were not born and raised as noble-women and how ladies dealt with the whole matter was something he really did not wish to think on.

But think on it Giles did, even as he stopped in the smaller chamber and pulled his braies, shirt and tunic on, tied his stockings up and then his boots. Buckling on his belt and scabbard, he realised that Fayth did not play the high and mighty lady-of-the-manor here. Her role as steward was a temporary thing, and then she would go back to doing whatever ladies did. He slid his sword into its leather carrier and his dagger into his boot.

What *did* ladies do?

Thinking back to his time fostering with his Lord Gautier, he remembered his wife sewing and embroidering, seeing to the state of the keep and those who lived in it, and praying. Lady

Constance prayed much. And so did the ladies who attended her. But most importantly, they saw to their lord's comfort.

He reached the hall and took his place at table, waiting on the light fare they ate in the morn. His men and those who served him entered, ate at the other tables and left to their duties. Giles waited to see if she would come down to eat before seeking out Roger and Brice with orders.

Finally she entered and he watched her every move as she walked from the stairway and made her way along the hall to the front. A soft smile here, a word there, to anyone who met her gaze or offered a greeting. Then he realised what was missing—Fayth had no companions other than her servants. Any other noblewoman he knew of or had seen always had a gaggle of other women around them or were in a gaggle of women around another woman.

Fayth was alone.

At the time of his arrival, he had isolated her on purpose for her safety and his peace of mind. While she had recuperated from her injury and while he had been still not certain of her motives or actions, it had been easier to keep her in her chambers. Once married, he had been unhappy with the thought of her wandering around the manor unescorted and unobserved. When he had assigned Brice to aid her, he had given her need for companionship no thought for he knew that Brice would protect her.

He had never looked to her comfort or care. Until now.

He stood as she drew close and assisted her to a chair, holding onto the hand he claimed as he aided her in sitting. Once more he wished that he could see more of her, for her Saxon dress prevented him from seeing enough to know if she was still pale or not.

'Where are your ladies?' he asked without prelude. 'Did none live with you to share your company or foster with your parents?'

'Good day, my lord,' she said quietly, but nonetheless he felt the rebuke over his haste. But she did not remove her hand from his, so he took that as a good sign.

'Good day, Lady Fayth,' he said. 'Are you well?'

'I have no ladies, my lord,' she said, ignoring the question about her health. Just as well since there was nothing more he could ask or say on the matter.

'When your father was lord here, did no one serve as companion to you?' Finally releasing her hand, he picked up an apple and cut it in two, offering her a piece. She shook her head, accepting only a cup of ale from the serving woman.

'Two of my cousins stayed here, my lord. One returned to her parents' home to be married and the other was called home before the king went north.'

'So you have been here alone since that time?' She nodded. 'And your mother? When did she die?'

'Two years ago, of the fever,' she answered.

'I do not mean to probe in old wounds, lady. I seek a way to aid you in your position here as my wife. Is there some other cousin you would like to invite here? Or I could send to my friend, or rather his wife, to see if she knows of any suitable companions—if you were to permit it? Lady Elise always seemed to have an overabundance of women surrounding her.'

Part of that, he knew, was due to the presence of the three men who served her husband. Mostly due to Soren, but many others were attracted to him or Brice or even to Simon before his recent marriage.

'I cannot think of one right now, my lord.'

Of course not. With war raging she probably thought him mad. 'When things settle, think on it. I am not opposed to such an arrangement.'

He let her eat, or drink for she sought no food this morn. The aftermath of her stomach illness most likely the cause.

'Did something untoward happen in the village yesterday?' he asked.

He could not bear to see the fear in her eyes and could not explain it to himself. Their last encounter had been one of passion and pleasure, freely given and accepted, but had her doubts risen once he'd left the keep? Did she worry once more on her guilt for placing herself under his touch?

Was this why married men sought out others for their pleasure, leaving only the need for children between them and their wives?

Nearly every man of consequence he knew kept a leman for their pleasure, not just noblemen but also others who were high in the esteem of their dukes or counts, knights and landowners on the same level as he was now. They went from their wives' beds to their lemans' arms, sometimes in the same night or sometimes for days or weeks at a time. After planning a new keep for the area near the fork in the river, he thought that it would be easy enough to have his lady wife there and keep a leman here for his visits.

What was he thinking? Truly, he was going mad. Glancing at the lady now, he knew from the moment her eyes had met his, even as she had pleaded for another man's life, that she was the one woman he wanted. He wanted her in his bed, under his touch, at his table and in his keep. He wanted her to bear his children and to grow old with him.

He could blame it on losing his senses in the battles he'd fought or from too many days in the rain or on many other circumstances, but none of that mattered. When he'd allowed himself to dream, sitting in the rain, looking at the hill that would become their new home, he had seen her at his side. Truly, he wanted no other.

Fayth tried to form an answer to his question, but got caught up by the curious light that entered his eyes just then. It was as though he were noticing her for the first time and finally taking stock that he had a manor and lands and a wife.

She remembered waking briefly in the night and thought she remembered him climbing into bed, but the sleeping herbs in Emma's posset had fogged her mind. Upon waking fully this morn, wrapped and warmed by his naked body surrounding hers, Fayth had simply lain there, enjoying the comfort he provided. If anything bad was to happen between them, that moment and this one were what she would try to hold on to.

'Was it memories of your father again, Fayth? Did it bother you being in the village?'

For as merciless as he'd first appeared before her, sword in hand, fighting his way through her men to get to her, it seemed a distant memory now after the smaller things he'd done. Easing her people's way. Protecting them from danger. Now, this concern for her comfort and her pain.

And all the while, she intended to seek out

his enemy for proof of his involvement in her father's death. Even while she planned to aid his enemies if they needed her help. She had not missed the sack of food that Edmund had carried into the weaver's hut with him—they were pilfering from the keep's supplies.

'It was sad memories again, my lord,' she answered honestly.

'Did you see something in the weaver's cottage that caused it?'

Fayth tried to keep her breathing slow and steady as she heard his words. Did he know about Edmund, then? Did he know she'd met him there? Had Brice seen more than she thought?

'Brice said he returned there and searched it after placing you in Emma's care and could find nothing.'

Pray God, Edmund had escaped first! She slipped her hands under the table and clenched them tightly. She must give him some answer and then she remembered the last task she did and nodded at him.

'I found a parcel of fabrics my father had bought at the summer market. I had not seen them before, but they were stored there and I came upon them. It upset me more than I expected.'

'Would you rather I withhold my permission for you to go there? Would you rather I order Brice to see to things in the village while you oversee the keep only?'

Yes! Her mind screamed out the word. If she could not go to the village, she would not be forced to make the decisions that seeing Edmund would force on her. Like a tempted soul, she would not sin if she had not opportunity to do it.

She must be strong. She must find out the truth from Edmund and she must help those of her people that she could and if that meant giving them some spare food to get them through the coming winter, then so be it.

Even as she opened her mouth to say the words, her heart was not in it. Her heart saw this man trying to see to her comfort. This man being a better one than those higher in rank and wealth. This man who terrified her and frightened her and at the same time made her feel alive and valued.

'I would not shirk my duties because they're difficult, my lord,' she answered. 'We are almost done there and should only need another day.'

'Very well, then,' he said, rising from his chair, his gaze still intent and yet different.

'Brice and I will be working in the yard when you are ready.'

'I have some numbers to add to the records before I return there,' she said. 'It may take me some time.'

'Worry not,' he said as he gifted her with a smile that spoke of wicked plans. 'By the time you are ready, he will beg you to remove him from my swordplay.'

She watched as he strode off, intent on besting his friend in practice. Fayth noticed the fraying edge of his tunic and the torn sleeve hanging down. She had been remiss in seeing to his care and his needs since he'd given her duties back to her. Planning to inspect his clothing chest to see what he needed later, she turned her attention and efforts back to the task at hand—the scrolls.

An hour or more had passed as she worked on completing the inventory of foodstuffs and supplies within the keep and those she'd found in the village. Other than a few cheers coming from the yard that shook the keep's wall, she worked in the silence of the hall. Then a commotion in the yard began. Not knowing, she gathered up the records, carefully rolling and binding them before returning them to the steward's closet. By the time she'd finished, Roger was leading a small group into the hall.

'My lady,' he said with a bow of his head, 'these are Lord Huard's men and Lord Giles asked that you see to them until he can arrive.'

With a nod, she called to the servants for ale and then watched the four men approach. They did not walk so much as swagger, all the time saying things under their breaths to each other that she was certain she did not wish to hear. One even had the audacity to touch her as he passed her. Soon, they were seated at the table, drinking ale and talking amongst themselves.

They did not realise or care that she could understand their Norman tongue. She felt her face flaming at their lewd and vicious comments and just when she thought she could not stand another word Giles entered from the yard.

Tempted to run to him, she stepped away from the table and allowed him to greet them on his own.

'Sir Eudes, welcome to Taerford Manor,' he said. 'How can I be of service to your lord?' Giles's greeting seemed appropriate to her, but the men at the table guffawed loudly instead of accepting it.

'Oh, how the lowly have stepped up, eh, *Lord* Giles?' Sir Eudes said. 'Stepped up too high, if you ask me.' Shocked, she waited for Giles's reply.

'Ah, but the duke asked neither you nor your lord for their opinions in this, did he, *Sir* Eudes?' Giles took a cup of ale and drank it down. 'So, what is it that you or your lord wants of me?'

Like a group of young boys who lost their concentration and rolled on the floor like puppies, these men did the same. They seemed to take notice of everything in the hall, or every person, and commented on it to Lord Giles instead of answering his question. Then they all turned and looked at her.

'Looks like you got yourself one of the pretty ones, did you not, Lord Giles? Lord Huard was left with two old Saxon cows with teats down to their waists and one too young to be ridden well yet, if you gather my meaning,' Sir Eudes leered.

'But how can you tell when they cover themselves like that?' He pointed at her and she backed away until she reached the wall and could go no farther. 'If you take them in the dark, you do not need to see them or their faces to plough them deep, do you, my lord?'

Because she was looking away, she did not see Giles move, but the crash of the knight to the floor and the movements of Roger and the other soldiers into the hall drew her attention. With his knee on Sir Eudes's chest, Giles held his dagger at the man's neck.

'That is my wife and you will not speak of her, or like that, in her presence,' he demanded. At the knight's hesitation to agree, he pressed harder until he succumbed. Giles pushed him away with his foot and placed his dagger back in his boot. Fayth noticed that many of Giles's knights and men now surrounded the group at the table.

'As I said, tell me your business here and be gone.'

Sir Eudes stood then and brushed himself off, holding on to any answers he would give. When Giles took a step towards him, he started to speak.

'Some of the serfs bound to Lord Huard's lands are escaping and he wants your word that you will not allow them onto your property. He sent me to make certain you understand what's expected of you, with you being a—' the knight paused then and Fayth wondered if he would have the nerve to use the word '—a bastard knight, and not raised to know how a true lord behaves.'

Stunned by the audacity of such rudeness, Fayth held her breath and waited for the fighting to begin. Instead silence filled the room as the men waited on Lord Giles's signal, for surely he could not let the insult go unanswered. He walked alone over to the other knight and stood so close she could almost not hear his words. His knights closed the circle around the others, significantly outnumbering them and making certain they knew it.

'A Breton, did you not mean to say, Sir Eudes? I may not know Norman ways because I am a *Breton*?'

Although rough and rude, Sir Eudes did not act the fool and his nod and agreement showed that he knew the odds were against him. The vicious look in his eyes told her he would not forget this insult by someone he considered below him in rank and privilege.

'A Breton is what I meant,' he mumbled.

'What you meant…?' Lord Giles pressed the point.

'What I meant, my lord,' the knight spat out more loudly.

Lord Giles stepped away then and nodded. 'Give Lord Huard my regards and tell him I understand my obligations to my Norman neighbours. Roger, Lucien, escort these men to the edge of my lands so that they do not lose their way.'

His commanders and six other knights led the others away. Giles, Brice and a few others stood together whispering and arguing furiously, but every few moments another expletive or curse rang out from them. Clearly these two groups of men hated each other and their disputes went back to their homelands. There was more at play than a simple message from one lord to his neighbour.

Unwilling to disturb them, but unable to move unless she did so, Fayth waited until they remembered her presence, trying to pick up fragments of their conversations. It took but a minute or so before Giles glanced over at her and issued some orders to his men regarding her. He left them and came to her side.

'I cannot allow you to visit the village today, lady. I would take no chances with your safety or give them the opportunity for mischief of any kind against me or my people.'

'I understand that his insult against me was against your honour, my lord, but I thank you for defending my person to him.'

'You are my wife, lady,' he said, lifting her hand to his mouth and kissing it. 'I would defend your honour to any man.'

The devil tempted her to her next words, and she could not resist asking it. 'Am I fortunate that Sir Eudes did not arrive a few days ago when you yet believed I'd given mine away?'

Instead of the anger she expected, a chagrined expression filled his face and he nodded to her.

'Aye, you are correct and I fear that I demanded your trust in me without giving mine in your word, Fayth,' he said in a low, private tone to her. 'I only ask that we will speak on that matter in private before we speak of it in public,' he said. 'I would rather have any wifely reprimands delivered away from the eyes of my knights who would taunt me later on my numerous faults if I give you leave to do so before them.

'For now, though, my lady, I will assign Emma and the girl to you to assist you in any work you have here in the keep.'

She nodded in acceptance, for he'd surprised her beyond words once more and Fayth waited for him and the other knights to leave. Just before he left with them, he returned to her.

'You are still very pale, whether from the rude words you suffered or from your illness matters not to me. If you feel the need to rest or to walk outside in the air, please do so and do not overwork yourself until you have regained your strength.'

He'd saved her from betraying him this day and she accepted it. When Emma and Ardith arrived, she decided to see to his clothing. It took the better part of the afternoon to sort through his meagre selection of tunics, shirts, stockings and breeches and to alter some of her father's to fit him more closely.

The knights and others in the hall were quiet through their evening meal and there was none of the usual frivolity amongst them as they ate. Mayhap the work was wearing them down, mayhap it was something else? Whatever the reason, she found herself in her chambers along with her husband earlier than was their usual custom.

Chapter Fifteen

Giles carried a cup with him when he entered and handed it to Fayth as her maid had directed him to do. When the old woman got that look in her eyes, he thought it best to do as she ordered. He smiled as he remembered that it had ever been so between them since his very first day here in Taerford.

'A posset to help you rest. Emma said to drink it as you ready yourself for sleep and not before,' he repeated the instructions to her. Sniffing, he grimaced from the odour of it. 'It smells…' He could not find the words to lie about it. 'It smells like pitch and mint.'

Handing it to her, he walked away, shaking his head over how anything smelling like that could be worth the taste endured in swallowing it.

Fayth put down her mending and took the cup, smelling it and nodding in agreement. 'Would you rather I slept in the other chamber this night, my—' she paused as his gaze narrowed in warning '—Giles?'

'Why would you do that?' he asked, completely confused by her question.

'I have heard that men do not wish to share a bed with a woman who…' She could not say whatever words she meant to say.

'Who drinks a putrid brew that makes her breath stink?' he finished. It brought a smile to her face and that pleased him somehow.

'Women who suffer their monthly courses, Giles,' she finally admitted.

'Ah, just so. Are they contagious in some way, then?'

'Nay,' she said, her smile turning into a laugh. 'You cannot catch them.'

'Then I see no reason to sleep elsewhere this night.'

He watched her as she pushed the needle through the material she sewed. The pile next to her held five or six garments, all of which looked very familiar to him. She was mending his clothes.

'Are you going to sleep in your clothing, Fayth?'

His question clearly startled her at first, then she shook her head. 'Nay. I was but waiting to learn where I would sleep before removing any of it.'

Giles took the chance and walked over to her. 'May I?' he asked as he touched her veil, a nuisance he wished removed as soon as possible.

At her nod, he lifted the circlet holding the veil in place and then unwound the length of it from around her neck and let her braided hair tumble free. He took the end of the braid, untied the leather strip and loosened the tightly woven braid until it curled around her shoulders and face.

'Does that not become uncomfortable? I would think it would retain heat and bring on a sweating.'

'Fashion has little to do with making sense, Giles.'

Thinking on some of the clothing and accoutrements he'd seen at William's court and other noble houses in Normandy and Brittany, he did not doubt it. Before he thought on it, he reached over and took the comb from the table and began running it through her hair. His hands itched to touch it so, and he finally had the opportunity. She sat beneath his hands, eyes closed, her breathing low and even, and he wondered if she'd fallen asleep.

'You are better than Emma at this,' she said. 'She pulls too much when there are knots or snags.'

They sat in companionable silence for a few minutes and he decided to broach another subject with her. He'd brought his sharpening stone and sword with him and so he placed the comb down and took the sword and the stone and sat in the corner, leaning against the wall.

'I had thought to knock this wall down and open up both chambers to our use. What think you?' he asked while sliding the stone along one edge of the blade.

'To what use would you put it?' she asked, standing then and gazing around the chamber as though judging it.

'Nothing more than to give us more room in

our chambers. It becomes crowded with only two of us in it and I would like my armour here as well. I thought a dressing area in one corner, with our trunks. A small sitting area here and the bed just there.' He pointed to the places he considered best and she turned to them as though imagining how it would look.

Her hair floated around her as she did, the length of it nearly reaching the floor as she moved to and fro. Giles put the sword on his lap and the stone next to him and watched her. His hands itched to wrap themselves in it, and he would once he claimed her as wife. For now, he took a deep breath and released it and focused back on his true task.

'I think it is a waste to do more than that here, lady. But I have plans to build a new keep on a hill near the fork in the river.'

'I confess that I've been hearing bits of this from your men. Why did you choose there?' she asked. He stood before answering her.

'That hill is suitable for the Norman style of motte-and-bailey tower keep. Using the hill, I avoid the work of building the motte first. Have you climbed the hill of which I speak?' She nodded. 'The view of the surrounding lands is clear and you can see for miles. A much better defensive position than this one.'

'And to what use will this keep be put?'

'Does it upset you to know you will move from the place where you were born?'

''Tis a woman's lot in life to leave her parents and cleave to her husband, so it comes as no surprise to me. But do you plan to level this one?'

'There is much I have not decided yet. Much depends on how quickly the trouble subsides and how we come through this winter. And,' he said, reaching over and handing her the cup, 'how many coins I have left after we buy what we must for the winter.' He urged her, 'Drink this. Seek your rest.'

When his wife did not take it, he placed it in her hands and backed away. 'I do not want to face Emma's wrath for not having followed her instructions. If you have any pity on me, you will do as she said.'

The smell of the brew was so strong he could almost taste it as she drank it down. He shuddered as he watched and waited until she'd finished to take the cup. Without asking her permission, he lifted the tunic over her head and then turned her to untie the laces at her back.

Somehow this comfortable banter and time of ease between them felt right. He'd never spent much time in a lady's bedchambers. Those ladies who would allow him entrance wanted him done and gone quickly. And the women who were like him, of the lower ranks or amongst the servants of the households he'd served, usually did not have a bedchamber to use.

Against a wall, under a wagon, in the stables or barn, even in the kitchen and laundry room of one lord's house, wherever there was a moment of privacy and a willing woman, he'd used it to seek pleasure. Never had he allowed himself to dream of a time when he would share a chamber with a lady as his wife.

She slipped the dress off her shoulders and stepped from it, leaving only her shift on. Before she could climb into bed, he took her in his arms and kissed her as he'd wanted to do since he arrived home last night.

Home?

The thought made him smile, but when his lips touched hers all thoughts of laughter fled his mind, replaced with the desire for her that always simmered within him, just below the surface of his control.

Giles ran his fingers up into her hair, holding her close that way and kissed her mouth over and over. Then he eased back and released her. 'I would hold you,' he whispered.

When she nodded, he stripped off his clothing and placed his weapons down in seconds, following her into the bed. He lay on his side and opened his arms to her and she moved into them. In but a few minutes, the posset did its work and she slept.

Home.

The word echoed in his thoughts until he, too, fell into sleep's grasp.

Fayth woke to an empty bed and an empty chamber. From the light that managed to force its way through or around the wooden shutters, she could tell the day was a pleasant one. Made even more pleasant by the absence of her courses.

With Emma's help, she dressed and sought her husband in the hall. She hoped he would allow her to visit the village. Listening to his plans, she'd begun to doubt Edmund's claims about him. She'd seen his outrage at Lord Huard's men and their demands. She would get word to Edmund and tell him that she could not help him.

She arrived in the hall in time to witness a loud argument between her husband and his friend. How they remained friends she knew not, for this was not the first nor the worst she'd seen between them.

'None of us have the least amount of knowledge or skill to handle this, Giles. It must be her,' Brice argued.

'And you have heard my word on the matter. The lady does not leave the keep this day.' At Brice's loud curse, he continued, 'You saw them and you heard them. The boundaries of my lands are but an imaginary line to them, there for them to adhere to or ignore at their pleasure. Huard will not honour it if he believes I have something of his and he believes it now.'

'Giles, be not an ass,' Brice yelled. Fayth

waited for the blows to rain down but they did not. 'This woman is in a bad way. 'Tis said your lady has some skill in these matters. I am not saying to let her traipse madly along the village paths, just let her see to this.'

'One of the women in the village can see to this, not the lady,' her husband declared, crossing his arms over his chest to signify the end of the discussion.

'May I have some say in this matter, my lord?' she asked as they all turned to face her. Apparently they were so wrapped up in their argument that no one had noticed her arrival.

'One of the villagers has been injured.' Giles looked at Hallam.

'Nissa, my lady. Wife of Siward the farmer,' Hallam announced to her. Hallam had come from the village, one of the overseers of it for her father, and had been helping with her work there. But the names he now gave her were none known to her amongst her people. 'They live with her sister, Edith, one of the weavers,' he prompted.

Something was afoot, for these people named were not tenants or serfs here. In remembering her husband's concerns about staying out of Lord Huard's matters, she realised the truth of it—they were runaway serfs from his lands seeking refuge.

'I know the woman you mean, Hallam. How is she injured?'

'Her sister would only say that she is in grievous pain, my lady.'

She looked at her husband and waited on his judgement. If she pushed for permission, she was certain he would refuse, so she crossed her own arms and tapped one foot and stared at him. It was a gesture her own mother had used frequently in dealing with her father, so she thought to try it now. Apparently, it worked, for he let out a curse that made her cringe and then shouted orders that made it happen. He left the rest in Brice's hands and did not accompany them.

After gathering what Emma thought best to take, they made their way under guard to the village and to Edith's cottage. When Brice would have entered first, she stopped him.

'If this is a womanly injury, surely you do not wish to help, Sir Brice?' she asked, gifting him with the most innocent expression she could force. Men rarely wanted to involve themselves in 'womanly matters'. When he withdrew, she followed Emma into the hut and found the woman in question on a pallet by the fire.

Fayth could see no place on the woman that was not burned or bruised. Her hair had been roughly chopped nearly to her scalp in spots and her lips were torn and bloodied. Fortunately, she was unconscious and did not feel the ministrations of those called to see to her.

'My lady, can you help her?' Edith begged.

'Emma is the skilled one, Edith. Let us assist her and see to your sister's needs.'

Emma listed the items she needed and Fayth watched as Edith moved quickly to get them. Fayth opened the chest of herbs and medicaments and mixed unguents and possets as she directed…and she tried not to let the horror of this woman's abuse show on her face.

The woman's husband could not hide his. She glanced up to see him standing in the corner, not in much better condition than his wife. She went to him to see to his needs. Siward brushed her off and begged her to help his wife.

'What happened to her?' Emma asked softly.

'The Norman lord did not believe that we were free tenants and he had us beaten when we dared to argue.' Siward let out a rasping breath, one that spoke of broken ribs and other damage. 'He took all the women and marked them as his slaves and then turned them over to his men. Nissa fought back and tried to escape and they…and they…'

'Hush now,' Emma said, passing a cup to him. 'Drink this and it will ease your pain.'

With efficient and careful movements, the three women washed Nissa and removed the burned and torn garments from her. Turning her on her side, Fayth nearly cried out as they witnessed the horror of her back and legs. She forced it back within and continued to work with Emma and Edith to finish cleaning the woman's wounds and dressing them.

It took some time, but finally they finished and were able to make Nissa swallow some of Emma's pain concoction before letting her rest. Siward didn't move from his place until they drew a blanket up around her.

'Refuge, my lady. We beg refuge,' he whispered.

'I cannot grant that, Siward. My lord husband is a vassal of the Norman duke and I do not think he will go against Lord Huard in this.'

Her heart broke at the thought that Giles would allow such injustice to happen and not intercede, but after Lord Huard's men had made Giles's place very clear, she simply could not answer for him. She was about to find out if Emma could stay with the woman, when Brice interrupted from outside.

'Lady? I need you to come outside,' he said, with enough firmness in his tone that she knew it for the order it was.

She placed her fingers to her mouth in a sign of warning to the others and then opened the door a bit and crept out, not allowing enough room for anyone to look in past her.

'Yes, Sir Brice?' she said, stepping a few paces off towards the path, thus making him turn away from the doorway to speak to her.

'Did I hear a man's voice in there?'

'Yes, of course you did. Nissa's husband—' she lost the man's name in her thoughts for a moment and then remembered it '—Siward watches over his wife.'

'How did the woman become injured? Are her injuries so serious that you were needed?' His eyes narrowed and she knew he doubted the story given.

The sight of Nissa's body upset her so that she could not piece together a credible lie to give him. Yet, she did not think she could trust him with the truth of it.

'Two days, Sir Brice. Give me, give them two days and they will be gone,' she pleaded. Grabbing his arm so he could not move away, she leaned over close and whispered so only he could hear her words. 'Those damn Norman pigs,' she sputtered. 'Those pigs…' The words would simply not come.

'Lady, do not get in the middle of something like this. And do not ask me to keep something from your husband,' he said, pulling free of her. 'You would do best to tell him the truth and let him decide his own part.'

'Sir Brice, my father rented out some of his lands just before he went north and without looking at the rolls, I could not say for certain if these people are on it or not.'

She decided not to let this happen. Given two days to rest and heal, Siward had a chance of escaping Lord Huard's men. If Edmund came back to the village, she could leave word for him to take them north with him.

'Lady,' he growled in warning, knowing the path she would take in this.

'It will take me time to search for the correct scroll and decipher the names and farms assigned by my father before he left. Just give me two days to read the rolls.'

She began to go back into the cottage to make arrangements with Emma when he took her by the arm and drew her close.

'Fayth,' he warned through clenched jaws, 'do not do this.'

Startled by the use of her name and the fierce expression in his eyes, she looked at his grasp and then at him with narrowed eyes until he released her. Fayth didn't think that he would harm her; he was just trying to make his point on the inadvisability of her actions.

'Of course, Sir Brice, you should feel free to

search the rolls yourself or ask my lord husband to do so if you want your answer sooner.'

The insult stung, she saw it in his gaze before he stalked off a dozen or so paces away and continued to call down curses on her head. Never once, though, did he force his way into the cottage and expose the runaway serfs himself. Fayth ducked back inside and spoke with Emma. In a short time, she was ready to return to the keep.

The knight sat on his horse, waiting for her when she left the cottage. Since it was only her, he leaned down and helped her climb up behind him. She could feel his anger, so she did not provoke him with words or questions while they rode back to the keep. Only when they passed through the gates did she dare to ask.

'What will you do, Brice?' she whispered from behind him.

'Since I was the one who convinced Giles to allow you to see to this, I have decided to honour your place as lady here and will allow you to handle this as you see fit,' he said.

She let out the breath she was holding, expecting him to expose her actions to her husband.

'My thanks to you…' she began, but he shifted in the saddle to look at her as he spoke.

'You will not thank me, nor will your lord husband, when this matter comes to light. And doubt not that a day of reckoning will come over it.'

'If he knows not—' she began and he interrupted yet again.

'You restrict his options and choices in the matter and give him no opportunity to act on his own to right things.'

Fear pulsed through her at his words. It was true, she was taking the decision out of his hands, but she did not believe that he would help this Saxon couple against their Norman lords. Still, she thought it was the right thing to do in these circumstances.

At least until Giles came out to the gates to greet her. As he walked forward Brice wrapped his hand around her arm to help her from the horse. His last words worried her the most.

'I pray God that my lady wife meddles not in my affairs the way you have chosen to do in your husband's. I fear I could not forgive a woman who did so.'

His anger frightened her and she stumbled as her feet touched the ground. In but a moment Giles steadied her with his arm at her waist.

'My thanks for seeing to the lady,' her husband said to his friend. Fayth could not meet the knight's eyes.

'I shall return, Giles. I need to ride.'

He pulled on his courser, causing the horse to rear up on its hind legs before landing forward with a great thud. Fayth moved with Giles to give the knight room and within a few seconds the knight urged his horse to a gallop and they were gone through the gates.

'Lucien, watch his direction and send two riders after him,' Giles called up to the guard tower.

Taking her hand, he led her along towards the keep. 'Worry not, lady. He suffers these dark moods and nothing can soothe them.'

'Nay, my lord. I suspect it has been my behaviour that has so angered him. I do not jump at his command or take his counsel when offered.' It was close to the truth.

'Lucien, where did he head?' he called out just before entering the building.

'To the east, my lord. I am sending Stephen and Fouque after him.'

'They are the best trackers amongst my men. They will make certain he returns in one piece.'

As she followed him inside Fayth realized that Brice was headed towards Lord Huard's lands.

Brice strapped his helm and sword to his saddle and gave his horse its head to gallop. He headed east towards Huard's lands to seek answers to questions he'd not shared with Giles. Suspicion was all he had right now and without proof he would not draw Giles into the middle of it. But after listening to the lady's conversations in the cottage, he knew there was more going on here and he would be damned if he did not cover his friend's back.

He slowed his horse down and rode for several miles until he nearly reached the end of Giles's lands and then turned northward along a stream and a small rise of hills. He found a small lake and stopped to let his horse rest and water. It was there that Stephen and Fouque caught up with him. Giles had sent no orders along, so he led the men up through the hills to the borders with Huard's lands.

It took some hours to explore but Brice discovered the sickening proof of Huard's despicable acts against his people. Three bodies lay close enough to a road to be seen if someone rode by, in a heap, so he suspected that they'd been dumped there after death. Examining them, he imagined that the two in the weaver's croft must have the same types of injuries.

As they searched the area near the bodies they found the hoof prints of large, heavy warhorses in the rain-soaked ground. Giles and he and their men were not wealthy enough to afford the prized destriers that noblemen could, destriers that left prints like these in the mud.

But, Lord Huard's men were.

Brice swore the other two to secrecy until he could inform Giles of his findings, then they buried the bodies beneath stone cairns and rode back to Taerford Manor. It was after nightfall by the time they arrived and he found that the lord and his lady had retired to their chambers for the night.

Deciding to allow his friend his night of pleasure in his wife's bed before revealing the information he'd gathered, Brice only hoped it was not the last one they shared.

Chapter Sixteen

She'd been skittish all day, ever since returning from the village and being the target of Brice's dark temper. His friend had these episodes frequently and it was best to let him seek relief as he had today—riding far and fast. It was almost as though he knew his days as an unencumbered knight were drawing to a close and his time as a lord with many responsibilities and duties drew closer. Brice wanted those things, as Giles and Soren did, but the approach of gaining that which they had dreamed of and never thought possible made them nervous and uncertain.

Giles had faced it on his way here to Taerford, but had had only a few days in which to tackle his fears and ready himself to take control. Not an easy task, preparing for things in a matter of days that others took their lives to do, but now, seeing Brice grow tense and irritated, he wondered if his experience had been the easier one.

Giles tried not to press his attentions too quickly, but now that the time was here he was skittish, too. He'd watched as Fayth said her prayers, sliding the prayer beads over and through her fingers, her lips moving but no sound escaping. And all the while, God forgive him, he'd thought of nothing but her naked body under his.

He was hard already. He thought that it had started at the slight nod she had given him during dinner to his unspoken question about whether her courses had stopped. She'd blushed, while his blood had rushed to his manhood and had never left it. Giles shifted from his place on the floor, trying to ease the tightness in his groin, his blade now sharper than it ever had been after this last hour of working the stone over its edge. Anything, anything to keep his mind off what he wanted to do to the lovely Fayth.

What he would do to her once they were abed.

He tried to look away when she glanced over at him, but he could not. She'd removed her veil and let her hair down once he'd closed the chamber door and now sat in only her shift and a robe that she'd found in one of the old chests of clothing that day. The worst part was knowing the beauty that lay beneath those flimsy coverings and even knowing the scent and taste of her skin.

Finally, finally she'd gathered the beads together and put them on the table, signalling an end to her nightly ritual. She stood then and poured some wine into a cup, offering it first to him and then raising it to her mouth when he shook his head. Giles watched as her hands trembled badly. He stood then and went to her, steadying the goblet so that she drank every drop.

'Are you nervous, lady?'

'Yes,' she whispered.

He poured more wine for her and waited while she drank it, hoping it would ease her fears. When he took the cup from her and placed it on the table, she looked at him.

'Will it hurt as I have heard?'

'I, too, have heard such things, but I fear I know not, lady. I have never bedded a virgin.'

Virgins were not for men such as him; they were only dreamed about by men like him. Virgins were too precious to waste on bastard sons, men who could only get as far in life as they could grab or fight their way to. Virgins were saved for men who deserved them and who were raised to have them as wives.

Now, gazing into her eyes, he hoped that he proved worthy enough to have a woman like Fayth of Taerford. He was going to try to be.

Giles left her for a moment and put out the candles in the chamber, leaving only one lit by the bed. He wanted to see her face as she cried out her pleasure this time. He'd purposely left only his shirt and breeches on and he removed them with an amazing speed now. He pulled the coverings loose, turned them back and then sat on the edge of the bed. He held out his hand to her.

'Come to me, Fayth.'

Giles knew he was asking for more than her body with his gesture; he wanted all of her and all that was hers to give. Now. The slight movement of her hand signalled a willingness, but her hesitation spoke otherwise.

'No more half measures between us, Fayth. Come to me and be my wife, support me in my endeavours, for our success and for our people.'

'It is too soon, I think,' she whispered, still not taking his hand.

'It is not soon enough,' he replied.

'You would offer the same allegiance you ask of me, Giles? Simply because I bled and proved my words to you?'

'I would trust you as my wife if you gave me your word, *oui,* your honour now proven by your blood.' He stood then. 'I wish it could have been otherwise between us and truly I wanted to believe your word, Fayth. I tried. You know it was a weakness from my past that I wanted proof before trusting you further.'

She watched him with uncertain eyes, yet he knew within that it was not the act that she feared. She feared the rest, what he asked of her.

'Trust me, Fayth,' he said. Lifting his hand out once more, he whispered, 'Come to me.'

That he asked her and did not force spoke

much to her of his honour. Regardless of his being baseborn, his actions did tell of his innate nobility. He had qualities that she'd seen go missing in many called 'lord', whether Saxon or Norman. And she stood before him, with betrayal in her heart as he begged for *her* trust.

'Giles, there is much we should say before—'

He pressed a finger to her lips, stopping her from speaking. 'There is much we could both confess about our pasts, Fayth. I am asking for your future, from this moment on.' As though he knew of her actions, he whispered, 'All will be well for we will make it so,' he promised.

She watched as he stepped away and sat on the bed. His body was pleasing to her and did not frighten her as it had before; even the proof that he was ready to claim her made her ache in places she had never known existed before he arrived. Fayth knew also that she wanted the life he was offering her. It had come about in the wrong way, but nothing could change that short of another invasion. He was here. He was her husband and he asked her, asked her, to join with him and be his wife.

Fayth reached out and took his hand, accepting all he offered in that moment. Even knowing that a day of reckoning would face her, she would trust him to see a way through it. Moving closer, she waited for him to take her.

'Kiss me, lady,' he whispered.

Fearing her inexperience would disappoint him, she shook her head. 'I know not how.'

He spread his legs and drew her closer. 'Then begin as we have before and learn the way.'

She stepped closer, between his legs, and leaned her face to his. Instead of touching her, he put his hands on the bed on either side of him and waited. She'd never approached a man like this before, so she imitated something he'd done and slid her hands into his hair and brought her lips to his. When he did nothing but accept it, she began to kiss the edges of his mouth, and then she nipped at his top lip and then the bottom one.

His body reacted, his manhood surged against her legs, but he did not move. Fayth used her tongue to trace over his lips and when he opened them to her she dipped inside his mouth as he had hers. Tasting him and sliding her tongue deeper, she found his and touched it. But when she thought he would taste her, he did not.

Moving closer, even leaning against his hardness, she pressed her mouth more fully to his and, when his tongue did meet hers, she suckled on it as he had done to hers. It was pleasurable and she discovered that with each suck or stroke of it an aching throbbed deep inside her. His taste and tongue filled her mouth then and he changed the kiss, taking control of her mouth even as she felt his hands moving over her body.

When she lifted her head to take a breath, she discovered he'd slid the robe from her shoulders. Letting go of his head, she let the robe drop. Before she could begin anew, he untied the laces of her *syrce* and opened it. She closed her eyes and waited for the touch of his mouth.

Her legs trembled as he kissed her breasts, licking them and nipping at them and then suckling one tip and then the other. She rested her hands on his head and slid her fingers through the length of his hair. When the sensations became too strong, when her legs gave out from the onslaught of feelings rushing through her blood, he lifted her and placed her on the bed.

She thought he would bring the covering over them, but he did not. Instead, he covered her with his body and took control of her.

His mouth moved from hers, onto her neck and shoulders, and every touch made her ache. When he took her breasts again, her body arched towards his, her woman's core heated and wet and wanting his touch there, too. Instead, he laughed and made his way down her body, sliding up onto his knees and not allowing her to move. When she reached over to touch his hardness, he pushed her hands away.

'Not this time, Fayth,' he said as he renewed his attentions to every inch of her.

It was hard to breathe now, hard to hold a thought, hard to do anything but feel, and feel she did. His mouth was on her stomach now and that place between her legs pounded as the ache grew stronger there. If he would only touch her there, ease the ache with his fingers, she could…she would… Tossing her head back, she released the moan that fought its way out.

'Please,' she whispered. 'Please,' she begged. He ignored her words and continued his path lower. When he spread her legs, she tried to hold them together. The candle's light might be dim, but he would see…there.

'Open for me,' he cajoled, his tongue and mouth now on her thighs.

Not sure of anything but needing him to finish this torture, she let her legs fall open. But he did not touch her there. He lifted one of her legs over his shoulder and pulled her closer. His mouth kissed along her leg, nearer and nearer, until she thought he must mean to…

Oh, he could not think to…!

And he did. Before she could protest such an indecent thing, he opened her with his fingers and then placed his mouth there. She tried to pull away, the intensity of her body's reaction scared her, but he held her with his hand on her leg.

'Be at ease, Fayth,' he whispered, not lifting his mouth from her.

When his tongue moved over the place that ached the most, she lost the battle and simply felt. Tongue, lips, mouth and even, she thought, fingers touched her there, sliding over and in, making her arch and pull from it, making her wet and making her want something that he held just out of reach. He found that same spot he'd used his fingers on before and now licked and even sucked against it until she felt nothing but the tension within her.

Something wound, tight and tighter, inside her, until she could not move and breathe. Then it released her as waves and waves of pleasure rushed through her body, easing and answering the ache. She moaned loudly and keened out some sound from deep inside. He moved then, but she cared not, her body wept its release as he placed himself over her.

'Fayth, look at me,' Giles ordered in a gruff voice. When she opened her eyes they were soft and her gaze dreamy with the pleasure he'd given her. But he wanted her to know the moment he took her and made her his. 'Wife,' he said as he entered her tightness and pushed through her maidenhead.

He knew when it hurt her, for her gaze cleared of the passion and watched him as he moved in and stopped, waiting for her body to adjust to his. He could pause only a few seconds, for his body, denied this pleasure, demanded more. He slid his hand beneath her bottom and lifted her hips and plunged in deeply, touching even as far as her womb. Her wetness eased the way now and her body gripped him as he thrust forward and slid back, over and over. He began to lose himself in the pleasure of being deep within her when he felt his seed ready to spill.

He tightened and he pushed deeper still, plunging in until he could go no further and held himself there. He emptied himself within her and moaned out his release, enjoying the feel of her tightness throbbing around him as he did so. When there was no more to give, he pulled himself out and lay at her side.

It took several minutes before he could catch his breath, and he feared looking too closely at her for either his lust would reignite or he would see disappointment on her face from the pain she'd suffered. He should have known that Fayth would react as he least expected her to.

'Is it always like that?' she asked as she rolled to her side and pressed up against him.

'Nay,' he answered, peering at her in the dim light. 'Each time can be different.' He reached out and wiped a tear from her cheek. 'Did I hurt you?'

She rubbed her eyes, wiping away any others before he could. 'A little, just as you…as you…'

Pierced her maidenhead. He shook his head and smiled softly. 'And the rest?'

He swore she snuggled closer to him as she replied. 'It did not hurt.' She leaned up on her elbow. 'Will it hurt each time?'

Giles watched as her gaze moved over him. When she moved her hand, he thought she meant to touch him.

'Nay,' he rasped out, both in answer to her question and as a plea for her not to lay her hand on him there.

His flesh responded as though she had, for it filled once more and rose up. Then she did touch it and it extended beneath her palm. He inhaled sharply at the pleasure and pain of her grasp. 'Nay, Fayth.'

He pushed her hand away and climbed from the bed. She came to him a virgin and he must see to her needs instead of simply rolling her over and ploughing her like a common whore. And, more importantly, she was his wife and he needed to have a care for her.

Her maid, knowing of his plans as most likely

anyone in the keep did, had left a bowl of herbs on the table and a pitcher of water heating near the fire. Pouring the steaming water over the crushed leaves, he gathered up a few cloths and carried them to the bed. Giles took her hand and eased her to the side and waited as she used the scented water to soothe and clean the area between her legs.

He then washed himself and watched as she went over to the chest that held her clothes. When she lifted out a clean shift, intent on putting it on, he shook his head.

'Do not waste your time,' he warned. 'I will have you next to me as you are now when we are abed.'

His bold words were made bolder by the reaction of his body. There was no fear there when she looked on him.

'And what about you?' she asked, glancing at his hardness as it now stood against his belly.

'I fear it will take more than once before the desire I feel for you is satisfied,' he promised. 'It stands ready for the next time. When you are not sore,' he assured her.

He'd pulled the covers up when she climbed

into his arms, turning her back to his front, as they'd slept these last few nights. Giles looked ahead at a long night of trying not to press his attentions on her in her state when he felt her rub her bottom against him.

'You are ready and I am not sore, Giles.'

He pulled her closer, holding her tightly and sliding his hardness between her legs. Her wetness already slickened the folds there and he slid himself into her.

She might not have ached then or for a while after, but later on in the dark of night she begged for mercy and he simply held her close as she slept, satisfied in a way he'd never known before.

Virgins were not for bastards like him. Heiresses were not for mercenary knights with no name. But he'd received both in his marriage to her, along with a siren who had no idea of the passion she held inside.

So, if he now held all he'd ever wanted within his grasp, why did his heart pound with fear?

Chapter Seventeen

The next weeks passed too quickly for Giles, for they represented all the good that he'd thought having a wife and lands and responsibilities would be. Fayth worked along with him and, in that time, supplies were accounted for, moved to and stored in the keep. Once the inventory was taken, she turned her efforts to restoring the keep to the home it had once been. The wall was removed and their chambers were expanded as Giles had suggested, and he used some of the additional space for a tub after discovering the many joys of a wife assisting her husband in his bath.

Those who lived in the village were permitted back to their lands and cottages when the attacks from the north stopped. He noticed a number of villagers, tenant farmers, returned once the area was safe and patrolled by his men.

He did not look too closely or ask many questions. He simply accepted their return and their pledges to pay rent as they had before. It was lax, he knew, but he needed farmers to care for the lands and the woods and, without connections, he would have difficulty finding many free men to do so.

Brice's reports caused him to search his soul and his mind for a solution to the problem and danger that faced them. Allowing runaways refuge was against the law and Giles could be punished, or even forfeit these lands, if he was found guilty of such a charge. But he walked the thin line, balancing between trying to be the honourable man Lord Gautier had made him and honouring the laws of his duke.

Brice finished his work with Fayth, for he was no longer needed as overseer as Giles had given his trust to her and did not need his friend to watch her actions now. Brice's restlessness increased as his grant of lands was delayed and he spent more of his time away from the keep than inside it, sometimes on Giles's business and sometimes on his own.

Fayth still visited the village, checking on the injured woman until she could be moved and following the progress of their weavers and tanners. Her visits seemed to leave her less haunted than those first ones, but her eyes were always duller when she returned.

She was reticent about their growing affection only in front of her people, and rarely did she take his hand or touch him outside their chambers, but once they entered their rooms nothing stood between them. She both accepted and gave during their bedplay and they discovered many ways to seek and find pleasure between them. And, if the tenderness he felt for her was something more than just the desire and fondness a man felt for his wife, he was not unhappy about it. He looked forward to the long nights of winter when he could keep her to himself and make her realise that she was safe with him.

The only darkness in their contentment was the presence of Lord Huard's men on a frequent basis. Eudes always asked permission, but he made all of the Saxons nervous and most of the

Normans and Bretons Giles had brought with him liked him little more.

He would show up reporting missing serfs and ask permission to search for them in the village. Giles had allowed it once, but even with his men standing watch over the process his people were handled roughly and a few injured. When Eudes and Roger came to blows over a not-so-sly insult, Giles denied him permission to enter the village.

Instead, Eudes and his men would sit on the road leading in and out of it and accost anyone travelling there. It took but a few incidents before Giles withheld permission for even that, and Eudes was restricted to travelling only to the keep and back to Huard's lands.

With the dislike and tensions growing between him and this Norman lord, Giles should not have been surprised when a group of men wearing the duke's livery arrived at Taerford Keep.

Giles had entered the hall when he received word that the duke's men waited for him. Roger stood at his back, his place now since Giles had appointed him captain of his guard. With Roger in charge of the men, Fayth in charge of the keep and Hallam newly named manor reeve, Brice spent more time on his own and gone from Taerford, as he was this day.

Giles moved forward to offer greetings and was surprised to find a bishop in his hall. Walking to him, Giles kissed his ring, the sign of his Holy Office, and then knelt for a blessing. When rising to his feet, he welcomed him, still not recognising the man or knowing what would bring a bishop there.

'My lord bishop, welcome to Taerford Keep,' he said. Holding his hand out to Fayth, who stood watching against the wall, he brought her forward. 'This is my wife, Lady Fayth.'

'Lord Bertram's daughter?' the bishop asked.

'Aye,' Fayth replied, as she curtsied before him.

It was not until the bishop looked squarely at him that Giles recognised him after all. 'Father Obert?'

Father Obert had been the duke's clerk and had handled all the details when Giles received his grant of lands.

'A bishop now?' he asked.

'A reward for my faithful service to God and King,' Bishop Obert replied, with a wink at him. 'Many are rewarded in the same manner, eh, my lord?'

Giles noticed the words used by the bishop and asked him as he led him to the table, 'Has William been crowned king, then?'

'Nay, I but spoke in haste. He has been at Canterbury these last weeks and will move on London soon.' He lowered his voice then, after noticing there were other than loyal Normans in the room. 'We must speak.' Giles dismissed everyone, but asked if Fayth could remain.

'Can she understand our tongue?'

'Aye, my lord bishop, she understands and speaks it…and reads it as well.'

'Send her away, Lord Giles. I would speak to you in private first.'

When everyone but he, the bishop and the other of the duke's men remained, the bishop bade him to sit and moved the soldiers away from where they sat.

'The duke has received complaints about your conduct here in Taerford,' Obert began quietly with little prevaricating. 'Serious ones about sheltering escaped serfs and not allowing another lord's men free passage through your lands.'

Giles tried to remain calm as he listened to the bishop. Obviously Lord Huard was unhappy that Giles was not respecting his wishes on how to handle the growing problem of managing serfs and villeins, and had appealed to the duke to force Giles into accepting his incursions onto Giles's lands.

'Since I played a small part in you gaining these lands, the duke thought I should be the one to investigate these charges.' Obert glanced up at him. 'The duke does not wish his nobles to be fighting amongst themselves when their enemies yet traverse England.'

'I have little liking for Lord Huard or his methods, my lord,' Giles admitted. 'But, I have done my duty to the duke and have taken this keep and these lands, holding them as he ordered.'

Before they could continue and Giles could offer any defence or even explanation of these charges, the doors opened and a large group of soldiers entered even as his and the duke's men tried to keep them out. Eudes stood in the front, forcing his way through.

'Did you ask him yet, my lord bishop?' Sir Eudes demanded. 'Or ask that traitorous Saxon bitch he married?' Eudes spat on the floor. 'Though anything she says cannot be trusted. A woman like that should be using her mouth for one thing only, I say,' Eudes began, crudely rubbing his crotch, 'and it's not talking or praying, my lord bishop.'

Giles was out of the chair, dagger pulled, before he even realised it. He did not intend to kill Eudes but he would wound him. Every time the man opened his mouth it was for an obscene comment, and now he seemed to latch onto Fayth as his target. It would not do to allow his insults to continue.

He'd slashed out several times and landed two punches on the man before the duke's men intervened and pulled them apart. Dragged back and tossed in his chair, Giles wiped his sleeve across his mouth and waited for the bishop's words.

'There was a more serious allegation made against you, Lord Giles.'

'What was that, my lord?' he asked. Seeing the knowing glint in Eudes's eyes, he began to worry.

'That you had one of King Harold's sons and heirs as your prisoner and you released him.'

Eudes laughed loudly then but Giles could say nothing in response. He'd suspected Edmund was more than Fayth's father's steward or man-at-arms, he'd even suspected that he was Bertram's liege lord here for Taerford, but had never expected the truth.

Did Fayth…? He never even finished the question in his mind. Of course, she knew. She'd begged for the man's life and, like the fool he was, he'd let Edmund go.

'Bring the lady here,' the bishop called. Two of the duke's soldiers stepped forward and nodded. Roger did nothing until Giles consented, which he did.

They waited in stifling silence for her to be brought to the hall. Would she admit to knowing Edmund or to her part in the deceit? He would have had him killed if he'd known. Rumours flew afterwards that Edmund had escaped from the battle early on and fled west with another son of Harold's to try to regain the country for themselves or to support Edgar the Atheling's stronger claim.

And he'd been here, within his walls! Within his grasp and released because of the glint of a promise in a woman's eyes.

His head pounded then and he walked to the table and poured a cup of ale. His stomach rebelled and he almost heaved, but the sounds of her steps coming down the stairs drew his attention.

'Lord Giles, I will handle this, if you please,' the bishop said, motioning him away. 'Sir Eudes, I will have you put out if you disturb this.' The duke's men moved behind the knight, ready to act at the bishop's signal.

Giles could not look at her as she walked past him to the place the bishop designated. He could feel her fear and he knew she had the right to be afraid, for her actions would be seen in the way of Norman law now and her place as a Saxon lady held no sway here.

'Fayth of Taerford, I demand that you only

speak the truth in answer to my questions,' the bishop intoned gravely.

'Is it true that the man who you were attempting to marry when Lord Giles—' the bishop started, but Fayth interrupted.

'If I might explain, my lord,' she said. 'If I could speak to my husband…'

Not knowing if she held other secrets and fearing what else she might reveal, Giles waved her off. 'He is Edmund Haroldson, is he not? Heir to his father, the late king and Earl of Wessex?' he asked in a quiet voice, already knowing her answer.

She glanced at the others in the room for but a brief moment, before meeting his gaze. 'Yes, my lord.'

Merde.

'But, my lord, let me explain,' she said, walking to him. At his nod, Roger seized her and pulled her away. The bishop ordered her to be taken back to their chambers.

'That cannot be the end of it, my lord bishop,' Sir Eudes called out. 'She lied and she must be punished. She harboured the duke's enemy and attacked his men. This one is too busy tupping her like a bitch in heat to be counted on to take the right measures.'

Eudes never saw the punch coming, Giles was moving before he even thought of it. Certain he broke the knight's nose and possibly his jaw, he found the sound of the bones crunching beneath his fist was wonderfully satisfying.

'That is one way of handling it,' the bishop said, drolly, with a glance thrown at the man now lying bloody and unconscious in the rushes on the floor. 'Get him out of here now.'

Giles ordered Eudes and his men to be taken outside his gates and kept under watch until the bishop gave orders otherwise. When the hall was cleared, he met the bishop's gaze.

'What is your pleasure, my lord bishop?'

'I think the easiest way out of this quandary is for you to capture Edmund and turn him over to the duke. Then no one need question your wife's involvement, or even yours, in Edmund's escape or whereabouts.'

Giles felt the blood rush away from his head. He'd not even considered that Fayth might know where the Saxon lord was now. How much of a fool had she played him for?

A very large fool was the answer.

'Can I offer you hospitality this night, my lord?' he asked, forcing himself not to call out her name to ask her to make the necessary arrangements.

'I would like that. If I am to answer the duke's questions, I must dig a little deeper than simply confirming one part of these complaints, my lord. Expect that I will accept your hospitality for several days at least.' The bishop stood. 'Did I see that you have a chapel here? Do you have a priest as well or should I plan to say the Mass tomorrow?'

Giles turned and looked at him then, surprised at such an offer. He'd known many clerics in service to nobles, but never had he known one who was actually pious, other than Father Henry. 'Father Henry sees to the souls of Taerford, my lord.'

'I serve God first. I still think of myself as a man of God, then a servant of the duke's.' Bishop Obert smiled then. 'I would visit with him, if you do not mind? Does he stay here?'

'Lucien will show you to the chapel and get Father Henry for you. His room adjoins it.'

Giles stood there as the bishop and two of the duke's soldiers left. Roger returned after placing a guard at Fayth's door and took the other soldiers outside where they could wait for the bishop's further orders.

All the while he fought the urge to go to her and either beg for the truth or throttle her for keeping it from him. Until he knew which course he would take, he decided it was best to stay away from her.

She saw no one for the rest of the day or that night.

Other than Ardith sent with a meal, no one entered the room. Alone, she sat while everything in the chamber, even the chamber itself, mocked her for her stupidity and lack of trust. The bed where they'd spent hours in pleasure and companionship. The chair where she sat while reading to him. The belt that had been his gift to her, made by his mother and kept for the woman he married, the morning after she'd... they'd....

Damn her stupidity!

Brice had warned her that day in the village

that there would be a reckoning and it was here now. Her lack of trust in her husband had brought this on them.

She just needed to speak with Giles. If she could explain her actions, he would see her reasons were valid. But, in spite of her sending requests to him with any servant she heard passing her door, he would not come to her.

That he did not spend the night with her was not a surprise, but it did hurt. How could they settle this if he did not speak to her? Or mayhap he did not plan to? Would he put her aside now?

She paced the room once more, looking out of the window and then listening at the door. Fayth had been up at sunrise and, after washing and getting dressed, she stood at the window once more, letting the gusting winds of late November blow on her. She had not really noticed the cold until Roger spoke of it from the doorway.

'My lady? The bishop asked if you would like to hear Mass this morning,' Roger asked.

'Will my husband be there, Roger?' she asked.

'Aye, my lady. Though it was your Father Henry's suggestion to the bishop that brought it about.' He nodded to her cloak. 'I am to take you to the chapel if you want to go.'

Fayth grabbed her cloak and Roger helped her place it around her shoulders. She followed him down the stairs, through the hall and out into the yard. The winds were brisk and she held her veil in place as they walked. When they reached the chapel, he escorted her to her place in the front and stayed at her side.

In spite of trying to be discreet, she looked for Giles there. The bishop was to say the Mass, a great honour for a holding as small as theirs, and Father Henry assisted him on the altar. By the time the Mass ended, she'd still not seen him. It was only as the others filed out before them that she saw him standing at the door.

He stepped in front of her before she walked out.

Fayth almost did not dare to look at his face; she could imagine the rage she would find there. He allowed Roger to pass them and she heard the door close behind him.

'The bishop and Father Henry trust I will not harm you here in the chapel and thought it the best place to talk,' he said.

She wanted to believe his words were meant in jest, but when she did dare a glance at him, the grave expression told her otherwise. She followed him away from the door and waited for his righteous fury to strike. The question, when it came, was said plainly and softly.

'Why?' he asked, staring not at her but off into the corner of the chapel as though he could not bear to look upon her.

Fayth was not certain of his question. She'd betrayed him in ways he knew—and some he didn't—and she could not think of how to answer. He turned to face her and it was not anger, but devastation that filled his eyes. He held his arms at his sides, opening and clenching his fists.

'I understand why you did not reveal his true name in the chapel. I would have killed him then without hesitation,' he said. 'But later… later…when things were settled between us, why did you not tell me the truth then, lady?'

'I did not think you would find out, Giles. Once he left, I did not hope to ever see him again. The pieces of news I learned about the effects of the invasion and the chances of Saxon victory convinced me he was gone.'

'But when you saw him?'

She gasped at his disclosure. 'Did you know?'

'Only in thinking back on your words did I realise you must have seen him. In the village most likely? And when I thought you were upset over memories of your father, you were really thinking of Edmund.'

She wanted to deny it, but she could not. Fayth wanted to drop to her knees and beg his forgiveness, but she doubted he would believe her to be contrite over her acts. Instead, she nodded slightly in answer to his question.

'So, since our marriage vows in this very chapel, you have lied to me, betrayed me, deceived me, stolen from me...' When she would have objected, she remembered the missing supplies that she had accounted for as well as those she knew Edmund took from the village. 'And stolen from our people. For what, Fayth?' he asked. 'What did you hope to achieve by your acts?'

He walked a few steps away and looked at her. 'A Saxon uprising? It will not happen. William will have England as his, and no inferior little group of rebels like Edmund's is going to stop him. Harold's army and all the major Saxon landholders were destroyed at Hastings, leaving no one to lead and no one to fight.

'So, did you believe Edmund's claim that he but needed a stronghold from which to fight in order to win?'

'How did you know that?' she asked. It was as though he knew all the things Edmund had told her to gain her compliance with his plans.

'One of your men, now sworn to me, thought it best to trust me, *trust me*, with that information. Edmund and his men had been spotted foraging for supplies and sending people into the village. Hallam thought I should know so that I could protect you and our people.'

Her heart broke in that moment. Her people, the ones she thought to free by protecting Edmund's presence, trusted this Breton knight more than she did, or more than she allowed herself to.

'You know that he will use you even as William did—if he cannot or will not marry you and use these lands to stage his revolt, then he will dangle you before someone else, to make them jump to his tune. And then he will dispense with you with just as little regard for your safety or happiness as my lord did.' He sounded exhausted then, his voice giving out as he spoke. But he took in another breath and looked at her. 'So, if not to win his war, why?' he asked again.

'I hoped…' she began, but the tears clogged her throat. 'I lost everything, everyone I loved. I thought he could restore the world I knew.'

Her words made her reasons sound weak, as weak as they were in truth, because she yet lived in the house of her birth, surrounded by the lands that had come down over generations to her parents and to her. Her children would stand to inherit them. She felt like a fool now, looking on the problems she'd caused with so little reason.

She realized that, once she'd known that he was a man of honour, she should have trusted him.

Even worse still, as she recognised the pain in his eyes as he waited on her explanation, she should have given him her trust along with her heart the moment she'd known she was falling in love with him. She staggered back and leaned against the wall as the import of her feelings struck then.

She had fallen in love with him. Even as she fought him at every turn. Even as she thought that Edmund was the answer to her problems and the plight of her people.

It was him.

Giles.

He protected her people. He provided for them. He challenged her abilities and demanded more of her. And he cared for her.

'Are you finally seeing what you have done?' he asked. 'Will you finally tell me the truth and tell me where he is?'

She shook her head. No matter that she loved Giles, she could not turn Edmund over to the Normans. 'I cannot.'

He strode over to her and took her by the shoulders, forcing her to look at him. 'If I do not find him and turn him over to the duke's men, the bishop will arrest me and turn me over. If the duke believes Edmund still lives and is using these lands to hide and wage war on him, he will bring his army through here and nothing, nothing, will remain.'

She tried to look away for the truth was horrible to consider. 'The next Norman lord sent here will not spend a moment worrying over the conditions of his people. He will be like Lord Huard, treating them worse than he treats his hounds.' He shook her then and pulled her close.

'If I fail here, your family ends. You will perish, for William will not even try to find someone to take you as wife, because you are expendable. And, if I fail here, Brice and Soren will never get their opportunity to even try as I have to make a better life for themselves.' He released her and stepped away.

'All we have suffered through our lives, all our work, the training, the fighting, the battles and the loss of those we held dear will be for naught if I fail here.'

He rubbed his face with his hands then and she read the same exhaustion from a sleepless night that plagued her, too. Then, Giles looked at her as though he realised some truth.

'Do you love him so much that you will save him over all else?'

'Nay!' she cried out. 'I do not love him in the way you think, Giles. I told you he holds no claim to my heart.'

'You told me many things, lady, and I am beginning to doubt every word I have heard come from your mouth.' He speared her with his stare. 'Pray God, Fayth, please tell me where he is. Help me try to make this work for all of us.'

Fayth looked away, not able to meet his gaze and refuse his request again. 'Betraying Edmund to you will not redeem myself to you, Giles.'

'You told me you would trust me, Fayth. In our bed that night, you gave me your trust and I believed you. Trust me now to see this right. Tell me where Edmund is.'

Her heart screamed at her to do one thing, while her mind and her honour told her to seek another path. In the end, she said nothing. She watched as his mouth became a grim, tight line across his face and every part of her husband disappeared as the bastard knight from days before came forward once more.

'Damn you, Fayth of Taerford,' he whispered to her as he passed her and left the chapel.

Chapter Eighteen

Fayth was released from her chambers later that day only because the bishop wished to examine the manor's rolls of tenants, villeins, supplies and goods and no one else could explain them to him. Not certain of his aims or his temperament, she spent the first hours just answering his questions about the lands, the crops, the woodlands, the river, the mill and the peasants who lived and worked for Taerford.

Giles walked through several times as the bishop questioned her there in the hall, but he didn't look in her direction and didn't stop. When it grew dark and it was time for their meal, she asked to be excused to her chambers, for she could not bear to see her husband so and know she was the cause. Worse, with a word she could alleviate his pain, but that word would destroy her lifelong friend, as well as her soul.

She sought her bed, their empty bed, earlier than her usual custom that night. Her litany of prayers offered no comfort and no hope to her and she gave up trying to repeat them. Climbing into the bed, she reached over to where Giles should be and rubbed the pillows as she fell asleep.

She did not remember what woke her from her sleep, but a candle sat on her table throwing shadows around the room and she leaned up to see what stirred there. The sound of his breath was the first thing she noticed and then she saw his figure outlined in shadows cast by the flickering light. How long he'd been there, she knew not, but he simply stood over her, watching her.

He'd done that before—when she was hurt during the attack on Taerford, he'd visited her in the night to see how she fared. Emma had told her of those times once she had recuperated from the injury. This was not that kind of visit, though, and as his breath grew ragged she could almost feel his anger pouring out over her.

He'd sworn never to take her in force or anger, but now she'd driven him to madness. The thought that she loved another so deeply that she would risk everything they had together tore his heart into pieces.

Ignoring her did not make it easier.

Confronting her had made it worse.

And drinking the bishop's potent spirits, offered in brotherly compassion, made him want her even more intensely than before.

Now he stood over her, wanting her, needing her and hating her at the same time. If she'd remained asleep or pretended to sleep, he would have found the strength to leave her alone, but not Fayth.

Nay, when she found him staring at her in the night, she lifted the coverings and invited him to take her. He did not even take off his clothes, only loosened his belt and lowered his breeches and climbed in on top of her.

His anger moved him then, increasing his desire for her even as he reached out, took hold of her shift and tore it down the front, baring her breasts to him. Then using the edges of it, he drew her up and possessed her mouth, touching his lips to hers, entering with his tongue. He gave no quarter as he moved over her, nipping the skin on her neck and shoulder and sucking on it to soothe and to mark it, so she would remember his touch when she saw them.

She made no sound except the soft gasps of passion—damn her! She should not allow this, but she did. Every moment he pulled himself back under control, she touched him or stroked him or kissed him back, inciting both more anger and more lust within him. Fayth whispered gentle words as he plundered her body, making her whimper under his touch.

When he gave in anger, she accepted it with gentleness. When he spread her legs and joined with her, she opened to him, softening under him and allowing him everything he wanted. When he tried to ignore her pleasure and see only to his own, riding her as deeply and as hard as he could, her body tightened around him and she cried out her release even as she milked him of his seed.

He collapsed on her, empty and still angry. Giles wanted in that moment to beg her forgiveness for such an act, but he was unable to even think of the words he would need. As he pulled out of her body he saw the tracks of tears streaming down her face.

He could stand no more.

Climbing from the bed, he tied his breeches and tightened his belt as he walked to the door. He glanced back at her, alone in their bed, and realised she had taken his anger and refused to let him hurt her. His hand was on the latch of the door when she whispered to him.

'I do not love Edmund,' she said, taking in a ragged breath.

He knew what she would say next. She'd just shown him by allowing him his anger, but he did not want to hear the next words, yet prayed for them.

''Tis you I love, husband.'

He leaned his head against the frame of the door and closed his eyes. At another time, he would have sought out those words from her, even begged her to say them. But now?

'Damn you, Fayth,' he replied and he stormed out as angry as he'd stormed in.

Giles made his way back to the hall where Brice sat waiting for him. Another cup of the bishop's spirits, brought with him for medicinal purposes, he'd claimed as he shared the brew with them, waited on the table. He lifted it to his mouth and drank it without pause.

Mea culpa, mea culpa, mea maxima culpa.

Through my fault, through my fault, through my most grievous fault.

She was praying for forgiveness as he took her.

Giles closed his eyes and pressed his palms against the pain.

'Did you swive her?' Brice asked.

'Aye,' he said, letting out a breath.

'I take it that the act did not rid you of your anger,' his friend observed.

If not for the matter-of-fact manner, he would have punched him for speaking of anything so personal. But then he, Brice and Soren had tupped their way into manhood together, so he was about the only person who could discuss something like this with him.

'She begged forgiveness and told me she loves me.'

By Brice's silence, he knew he was shocked, too. He poured them both another cup of the liquor and neither spoke as they drank it down.

'What will you do next?'

'After I beg her forgiveness?' Brice nodded. 'I know not, other than trying to come up with a plan to capture Edmund, get rid of Sir Eudes and Lord Huard and make my wife obey me in all matters.'

'I would wager that the first of those are more attainable than the last one,' Brice offered.

'Just so. Come, friend. Let us seek our beds, for the morning will arrive quickly and there is much for us to do.'

Brice went off to sleep in the barn with the other soldiers and he went back up the stairs. Giles did not doubt that she would allow him back in their chambers and even in their bed, but until they spoke on matters personal, and about Taerford, he would not ask it of her.

For tonight, he slid down against the wall outside their chamber and slept there. When the servants began moving through the keep, bringing it to life, he opened the door and hoped she would forgive him.

It was morning, from the sound of it, so Fayth opened her eyes and stretched her muscles while still under the coverings. She ached as she moved and then she remembered why.

Giles.

Closing her eyes again, she remembered him coming like a storm to her bed, fury in his gaze and making love to her fiercely. Fayth understood it came from his pain and she could not cause him to hurt even more because of her, so she had simply allowed him to take her. She had feared for a moment, when he had torn her *syrce* open, but then she had known he was more angry at himself than he was at her.

The rest of it had been no more vigorous than their most passionate bout of bedplay.

She sighed, wondering if speaking of her love at a time of such anger had been a good thing. Too late now—she decided to dress and face the day. Fayth pushed the coverings back and sat up.

And found her husband watching her once more.

His face could have been carved out of stone, so grave and hard it was. But his eyes gave him away, for there was such pain and guilt there.

'Can we speak now?' he asked quietly.

Giles stood and handed her a new *syrce* and *cyrtel*, so she hastily pulled them on. She would worry about the rest when they finished.

'First, I know you think you deserved what I did, but you did not. I promised you that I would never take you in anger and I broke my word when I did,' he said. He glanced at her then and looked away. His expression filled with guilt. 'Forgive me, Fayth,' he said. 'I can only give you my word again and pray I have the strength to keep it next time.'

'Next time? What do you mean, Giles?'

She'd convinced herself in the darkest part of the night that he meant to rid himself of his troublesome wife either by annulling the marriage or by shutting her away. He certainly had cause to do either—even the duke's bishop would support him, knowing of her deeds.

'Although I have never been married before, I have seen many marriages, amongst nobles and amongst peasants. Some are happy and smooth, some are troubled and unhappy and some are a mixture of all of those. I suspect that ours will never be smooth, but I do believe we can find some happiness between us.'

'I thought you would put me aside,' she said, sharing her deepest fear.

'I have thought of doing that. I asked for your trust and your obedience and you gave it, or so I thought. Now, it will take some work to begin to rebuild what has been lost between us.'

'What must I do, Giles, to show you that I want this?' She stopped then, knowing exactly what he would demand of her—he had already demanded it. 'Must I betray Edmund to gain your trust?'

He walked over and pushed one shutter open, allowing the sunlight and some cool air in. Gazing out of the window for a minute and breathing in deeply, he shook his head.

'If I demand that of you then I am no better than he. I want to believe that I am better than that. I've told you why I must stop him—it is up to you to trust me to handle it or to withhold the information and protect him.' He pushed the second shutter and shook his head.

'I will think on it, Giles,' she offered.

'There is not much time, Fayth. Soon the choices will be taken from me and others will see to it.'

He walked to the door then. 'I will send Emma to you, but I wish you to stay here today. Eudes is still at the keep and I want you out of his path. If the bishop wishes to speak to you, I will summon you.'

She nodded, knowing he was trying to protect her. She felt as though she wanted to say something more, but dared not upset the tentative balance they'd somehow achieved.

He left, pulling the door closed, and she collapsed back on the bed. She'd expected far worse, but a glimmer of hope pushed into her heart then. He did not force her to betray her dearest friend.

No, instead he simply asked her to do it, putting the burden on her. Now she understood what he meant about how being forced to do something lessened the guilt involved.

It would have been easier if he'd forced her. Fayth did not know if she was strong enough to take that step on her own.

Whatever her doubts were, by the noon meal that day she faced the consequences—and they were of the most horrible kind imaginable.

Chapter Nineteen

Fayth heard the yelling begin a distance away from the keep and grow closer and louder. Putting down the tunic she mended, she opened the shutters of her window and tried to find the source of it. Recognising the voices then, she knew that Sir Eudes was in the middle of whatever was happening. Standing on her toes, she leaned up as far as she could, but still could see nothing.

Giles had asked her not to leave her chambers this day, but surely he did not mean she could not go into the storage room next to their room. Opening the door to that room, she went to the window and looked out of it. Unfortunately, she could see everything that was happening from her place there.

Sir Eudes and his men surrounded a bound

and gagged man who lay twisted on the ground. As he struggled, to get up or to get away, she knew not which, they kicked him and pushed him down. When he fell on his back, she got a glimpse of his face.

Siward!

She nearly fell from the shock of seeing him there, but she knew that if Lord Huard captured him he would die a slow and painful death. Looking around, she prayed that Nissa was not caught as well.

Fayth needed to get down there, needed to stop this from happening. Giles must…he must… She paused for a moment and thought on what he could do.

Siward was marked as a slave, a serf, someone attached to the lord's lands and not free to move about. He'd been found on Giles's lands. As a Norman lord, Giles had to comply and allow the man's return to his rightful owner. With the bishop here, observing and noting everything for Duke William, Giles had no choice.

The thought made her sick. Fighting against the choking feeling, she knew she must do something. Opening the door, she rushed to the steps, but Giles's voice, asking her to stay within, came back to her.

A man's life was at stake, she decided in that moment, and she would have to face his anger later.

Racing through the keep, she ran to the steward's closet and grabbed one of the parchment scrolls that listed her father's tenants. She prayed there was a name close to Siward's that she could find to make the case to the bishop. Pushing her way through the growing crowd, she arrived in front of the spectacle just as Giles did. His anger was obvious when he noticed her.

'My lord,' she called out to him.

'Lady, you do not belong here. Return to your chambers now,' he ordered.

'My lord bishop, I have the rolls of tenants…'

He reached her then, caught her hand as she held out the scroll and dragged her aside, stopping her from saying anything more by squeezing her arm.

'Get you gone from here,' he ordered through clenched jaws. 'Now.'

'I can help in this,' she began.

'You are the cause of this. Now get back inside

and let me see to it.' She was about to do as he said when Sir Eudes called out to them and the bishop.

'There is no need for her records and lists, my lord bishop,' the knight said. He reached down and tore Siward's tunic and shirt open, revealing his skin. 'He is Lord Huard's legal possession.'

Skin into which the letter H had been burned.

Fayth gaped as she realised that it had not been done with one iron carved with the letter, but by applying a long one three times against his skin to form it. As the one on Nissa's bottom had been done. Before she could do anything, Giles whispered to her that all would be well, pushed her into Roger's arms and loudly ordered her taken inside. He walked off without ever looking back at her.

She would not have made it back inside or up to her chambers without help, and she barely made it even with Roger's assistance. Fayth knelt there on the floor until Emma came in and helped her to the chair.

She should have told him about Nissa and Siward. She should have told him about

Edmund and his demands for help and his plans. She should have told him.

He should have told her the truth about his hand in helping Huard's runaways, but for now he would have to try to find a way out of this.

Brice had come to him with his reports about Lord Huard's treatment of his people and the bodies he'd found. All Eudes needed was to find one runaway, dead or alive, on his lands and he could bring Giles before the duke's justice and demand that his lands be forfeit. An easy way to break his claim and Huard stood to gain them by proximity alone. Until now, they'd managed to get those who had escaped him to the relative safety of the rebels' camp a few hours from his lands.

Why had Siward returned? It mattered not now, for he was caught and Giles feared he would not have enough time or a way to help him escape again.

'My lord bishop,' Giles began without a clue as to what to say next. Eudes helped him.

'No, my lords, with this mark as proof, we need not wait on any decisions or scrolls. Raoul, take this—' he kicked Siward again '—back to Lord Huard's keep.'

There was no way that the rebels could take down eight mounted knights if they were alerted to this, so Giles knew he must even the odds somehow. Two they could manage. He walked over to the bishop to try to gain his help. Eudes was not going to make this easy for him.

'As Lord Huard's man, I would say it would be within his rights to search the rest of the village for other escaped slaves now that we found this one, my lord,' Eudes stated, staring him down. 'Should I send this one back to the keep with my men or should I search the rest of your village, *my lord?*'

Damn! He knew! The only thing Giles could do was capitulate and hope to get word to the others. He leaned in close to the bishop, informed him about his suspicions over the dead bodies—whether they were his or Huard's villeins mattered not—and asked that Eudes's men be limited if they were travelling unaccompanied across his lands.

For reasons known only to the bishop, the former Father Obert agreed and gave the orders.

Looking over the heads of the crowd, Giles found Brice, having arrived during this scene, and signalled him to move on their plans. By the time two of Eudes's men left Taerford, Brice had already sent his message to the rebels to intercept them.

The crowd dispersed and Giles went in search of Fayth. Emma was just coming down and told him of the lady's condition and he decided he would not upset her more now. With a word to Emma, he left the keep to find Brice on his return and to come up with a plan to find Edmund.

If only she could trust him.

Fayth lay abed the rest of the afternoon. Her stomach finally settled and she managed to keep some broth and watered ale down. She dared not leave the room lest Giles discover she had disobeyed him once again.

She considered her actions and realised that once more she had fallen head first into trouble. Before Giles had arrived, she had made nary a misstep, she had known her place and her duties and none could have called her incompetent. Now, she was nothing like the daughter of Bertram used to be. Not used to reporting her actions to anyone while her father was away, and not accustomed to asking for guidance, she had had her life turned upside down by this man.

However, these were dangerous times and never could she remember an action of hers resulting in someone's death until she'd fallen in with Edmund's plan. Now, in addition to the men who died fighting Giles, she must add Siward to the list on her conscience.

Fayth knew she must stop her rash behaviour and, if she was committed to her promise to Giles, she must trust him with the truth and allow him to choose the right course of action for them.

And that meant telling him where the outlaws' northern camp was, and where he would find Edmund.

She had no choice, too much hung in the balance. If Edmund had heeded her warning he would be long gone from this area, seeking his relatives in Northumbria or beyond.

Reconciled to her decision, she waited for

Giles to come to her so that she might prove her love and her trust to him. She'd nearly ruined it yet again, but she was certain he would give her another chance. He'd whispered all would be well to her and she could only hope it would be so.

Her head was still spinning from her bout of stomach sickness, so she lay back on the bed to rest. The sun was much lower and the room grew dark when she opened her eyes. This time the man who stood in the shadows of the room was not her husband.

The evening meal was laid by the time Giles could seek Fayth out to explain. The day had gone from bad to worse, then even worse, and each time he had thought to go to her another catastrophe had occurred requiring his attention. After the disastrous morning and then the incident with Siward, he'd been called to the training yards where a fight had broken out.

Like a melee, it had swarmed across the yard, men fighting with fists and kicks until just the guards along the walls had remained uninvolved. Since he could not use bows and arrows on his own unarmed men, he had had to wait for them to wear themselves out. Roger and Lucien were yet looking for the reason for the outbreak, but he did know that it involved Lady Fayth somehow, with some insults being bandied around regarding the debacle involving Siward.

And all of this under the watchful gaze of Bishop Obert.

The bishop strolled through the keep and yard, visited the village, spoke with Giles's men, the peasants, Father Henry and anyone else he saw. And he said nothing.

He'd intervened when Giles had asked about retaining Eudes, but otherwise he seemed to take no action at all, other than saying Mass each morning and joining Father Henry in other prayer devotions.

Would he be given a chance to defend his actions before the bishop returned to the duke? Giles wondered. And how much time did he have?

Giles climbed the stairs, intent on first explaining his actions regarding Siward to Fayth and then bringing her down to the hall to eat.

Her people, he was learning, became very nervous when they did not see her for several days
in a row, as evidenced on his arrival, and then
these last days. Hopefully her stomach ailment
had ceased, but then even he had felt the need to
empty his stomach when he had seen the marks
on Siward's chest.

Giles listened at the door, but he heard no
movements inside. Mayhap she still slept? He
lifted the latch and pushed slowly on the door.
The chamber was dark, no candles were lit and
it appeared that Fayth was not inside. Lighting
a candle from the barely burning embers in the
hearth, he looked around once more.

The room was empty.

He called her name and went to the storage
room next, but the other chambers on the same
floor were all empty.

Without raising an alarm, he moved through
the keep searching for Fayth, but there was no
sign of her. Now that the sun was down, there
was no way to search the village or the roads.

Dear God, he prayed she was not on the road!

Eudes had left for Huard's keep not an hour
before, and he could not even think about what

could happen if the knight came upon her alone. More likely, she was in the chapel speaking with Father Henry. Giles would not be happy that she disobeyed him yet again, but if it was to seek the good priest's counsel or to give her confession he would not object.

He alerted Brice and they made their way throughout the rest of Taerford Manor, finding no one who could remember speaking to her that day. On circling back to the keep and talking to all the guards, they still could find no sign of her.

Now Giles was really worried. He went back to their chambers and searched again with more candles and Brice's help. When he realised that the carved wooden casket that she kept her ribbons and other personal belongings in was no longer in her clothing chest, he grew more concerned. But when he found her parents' betrothal rings on the floor next to the bed, he was terrified for her.

If she'd left him, if Edmund had come for her while she believed her husband would take no action to help Siward and the others, and if she still believed him to be just a heartless Norman lord, she would not have left this behind.

Not willingly.

And while his heart pounded with terror at the thought of losing her, he also fought the fear that she would leave him for Edmund. No, she had said she loved him. Though the thought of a lady such as her loving a bastard knight such as him would have been impossible just months before, now he knew it could happen.

He needed to find her.

Chapter Twenty

Fayth was hungry, tired and hurting.

And her nose itched.

They'd been riding since he'd taken her from Taerford, using every hour of daylight they had to get as far away as possible from Giles. At least her hands were tied in front of her now, and one of Edmund's men held her before him in the saddle, instead of slung over it.

When she woke to find him in her chambers, Fayth did not know what to do. How he'd managed to get in without being seen, what he hoped to accomplish by his visit, and how he planned on getting out all became clear when the chaos broke out in the yards. Every man in the keep and the yard somehow became involved, either trying to stop the fighting or jumping straight into it. A noisy distraction initiated to cover Edmund's entrance and their exit from the keep.

But she'd fallen for the worst distraction of all: Edmund claimed to have a witness to Giles's murder of her father and claiming of his ring. He'd brought a second man in who told of fighting near her father at Hastings and seeing Giles attack and kill him from behind. Then, Giles did not, they said, simply remove the ring, but hacked off her father's finger to get at it.

Thinking to disprove Edmund's allegation for good, she retrieved the ring from Giles's chest and showed it to them. Sure enough the crack the man described was there. But her doubt of the man's tale must have shown on her face because he began adding details to support his claim, including something that made her only more suspicious—her father's location during the battle.

She realised, as one of Harold's vassals, her father would fight with the division from Wessex, nearest to Harold, second only in importance to his housecarls and the shield wall. And Wessex always fought to the left of his standard.

Giles had fought on his duke's left flank, nowhere near her father's position.

She knew they suspected she did not believe so she pretended to gather some things together until she could figure out a way to attract attention. Edmund noticed the box he'd made for her, so she began to stuff it in the sack with some clothes. But before she did, she slipped out the rings tied together and dropped them on the floor, pushing them nearer the bed so that Giles could find them.

Hoping he would understand her message, she turned to find the men ready with rope and blankets and, before she could fight them, she was gagged, wrapped, bound and tossed over the other man's shoulder. With no hopes of being heard over the fighting in the yard, she was spirited away before anyone could notice.

They made a brief stop at the outlaws' camp she had intended to tell Giles about before continuing on towards the north. She saw some familiar faces at the camp and suspected Edmund did not wish to chance one of them intervening in his plan. When Edmund handed her up to his man, she caught a glimpse of someone who looked like Siward, but that was not possible. That poor man was most likely dead now at Eudes's hands.

Now, hours and hours later, they drew to a halt in front of a small cottage and she was handed down like a sack of flour. Put on her feet for the first time in too long, she wobbled until she nearly fell. Edmund's man untied her hands and feet and unwrapped the blankets that held her.

The first thing she did was scratch her nose.

The second thing she did was run.

But the hours without moving her legs had left them painful and a burning ache filled them, making it impossible for her to take more than a couple of steps before she fell to the ground. Edmund picked her up and carried her inside, ducking through the door and placing her on a pallet in the corner. When she had rubbed and shaken the burning out, he handed her a skin of wine and accepted a torch from one of his men.

'Why, Edmund? Why did you bring me here?' she asked, trying to figure out where they were. She only knew they were far from Taerford lands. Pushing her hair out of her face, she waited for his explanation. After placing the torch into a holder on the wall, he took the skin and drank from it. Then he crouched down next to her.

'You are the key to saving my father's lands and mayhap even his kingdom, Fayth.'

'I cannot marry you, Edmund.' She shook her head, not wanting him to consider that as an option at all.

'I do not plan on marrying you, fair one. I had planned that when I made it alive to Taerford. I thought that holding your lands would be a good place from which to stage our resistance. But now there is someone to whom I have promised you in exchange for the coin and knights we need to push the Normans back.'

The words he'd used had been almost the exact ones Giles had used when explaining the foolhardiness of continuing to support Edmund. She was no more than a foolish woman who saw more in herself than the lands she brought.

'He will not allow it,' she said, believing that Giles sought more from her than only lands. She did not deceive herself that those lands had brought him to her, but now, now he wanted her.

'Better for us if he does follow, for that would remove any impediment to marriage if this promised Welshman is so squeamish as to have one. One marriage did not stop my father from pursuing his goals though, so do not hang any hope on that to bring this to a halt.'

She watched in silence as he moved about the cottage preparing for night. His men, after securing the two small windows and blocking the door, remained outside while he took a place inside. He brought her some cheese and bread and then the night settled in on them.

'You do not want to do this to me, Edmund. My father loved you as his own and thought you worthy of his trust.'

'And I loved him as a father when I was sent away from my own, Fayth. But now, I have the chance to regain what my family has lost, what England has lost, and to keep the name and house of Harold Godwinson in power here.' Edmund let out a breath and met her gaze for the first time during this debacle. 'This is larger and more important than either or both of us, Fayth, and I will not fail my father or his legacy by letting this opportunity slip through my hands.'

She felt tears gathering and was the first to look away. When she'd finished eating, he took the remnants of their meagre meal, tied the sack and stashed it by the door. He handed her a blanket and waited for her to settle before handing the torch back out to his men. Fayth heard him make his way to the wall and slide down it to rest there. A few minutes later, complete silence filled the cottage and she hoped she could sleep.

'You are the key to gaining what we need to fight off the Bastard's control,' he whispered to her. 'Even though I truly wish it was not like this, I cannot let Fitzhenry live or let you go.'

A shudder passed through her and Fayth began to offer up her litany of prayers. But now she knew not if she prayed that Giles would find her or that he would not.

Brice thought Giles mad for leaving before dawn, but he would brook no opposition to his plan. If Fayth's disappearance had done nothing else, it had strengthened his resolve to find and dispose of Edmund. With plans in place for the defence of the manor and its people if Huard's men should attack before his return, or if Edmund did muster forces against him, Giles left Brice in charge, with Roger at the ready.

He took only Stephen and Fouque with him to find her, as well as Brice's promise to aid her however possible if he should fall.

He reached the rebels' northern camp at nightfall and discovered that Edmund was several hours ahead of him, on the north road to Gloucester. Several men approached him and offered to help him in his quest to save her— men who had served her father or, like Siward, had benefitted from her kindness in some way. Although pleased by such offers and glad to see that Siward had escaped and made it here relatively unscathed, he knew that any more deaths in her name would destroy her.

Giles and his men rested a few hours and left before dawn's light. If Edmund headed, as Giles suspected he did, to Wales and his father's old enemies to try to form an alliance to regain control of England from the duke, the land would grow more arduous and challenging. Edmund would never chance taking Fayth into the mountains until day's light broke upon them.

So there was still time.

They found the cottage just as the sun was rising and Stephen reported on the four knights outside. Edmund would be inside with Fayth. But before they could get close enough, Giles discovered that rebels could indeed get the better of two, or three, mounted knights. When he came to, he found the three of them trussed like game on the ground in front of the cottage.

Edmund's rebel fighters had arrived behind them and took them unaware with little effort. So focused on finding Fayth was he, he'd forgotten to cover his back. Now, they waited for Edmund to decide their fate, though he had little doubt what it would be.

Fayth heard the men outside before Edmund woke, but dared not move off the pallet. So far, he'd treated her without cruelty, but she feared what lay just beneath the surface in a man as desperate to save his family and name as Edmund was. She had to stay alive and watch for the chance to escape.

Edmund woke then, and, after belting on his sword, he opened the door, looking out at his men. Then he just laughed, bent over at the waist until she finally left the pallet to see the source of his merriment. Nothing prepared her for the sight of Giles and two of his men, beaten and tied, on the ground there. She tried to go to him, but Edmund seized her and held her back.

She thought to follow him when he left, but she found the door barred from the outside and no amount of banging and screaming made a difference. Fayth knew he did not plan to starve her, so she waited for someone to bring her food and drink. Listening against the door, she heard nothing and it worried her.

An hour or so later, the bar was lifted and the door opened. The man who had accompanied Edmund to the keep entered and bade her to come out. She rushed out, expecting to find Giles there, but he was gone.

'Where is he?' she asked as the man hurried her up a path next to the cottage. Although she could see that more men had joined Edmund there, she saw no sign of her husband. When the man did not answer, she grabbed his arm to make him stop. 'Did Edmund kill him?' she asked, dreading the answer.

'See to your needs, lady,' the knight ordered instead.

Fayth found they stood at the banks of a small stream. Still intending to find where they kept her husband, she washed and drank hurriedly and saw to her other needs even faster, not trusting the man to keep his back turned. On their way back to the cottage, she saw them.

Tied against three trees, a short distance behind the cottage, sat her husband and his men. Other than a few bruises, they looked little worse for the wear. When she tried to make her way there, a rough hand on her arm stopped her. Handed a sack and forced into the cottage, she could do nothing against the strength of the knight.

Edmund came to see her, thrilled that he now held the Norman lord to ransom for the duke. His few moments of enjoyment ended when Fayth explained the duke's thinking in giving the lands to bastards with little standing. His face grew stern and dark as he realised his error in judgement. Fayth hoped she'd not cost Giles his life with her comments.

Before storming out, Edmund revealed that they would remain here for another day, waiting for the rest of his supporters and their troops. Then he would take her into Wales to bargain with one of the Welsh princes who'd promised his aid.

With nothing to do but wait and pray, Fayth began exploring her small prison. Other than the two small windows, too small even if not covered for her and her gowns to fit through, as well as the door, there was no way out. Sitting on the pallet, she noticed that the sun's light pierced through a worn section in the wattle-and-daub wall. Searching the cottage for some tool to use and finding only a small, rickety stool in the corner, she broke it into pieces, explaining to the guards that it had collapsed under her weight.

Using one of the legs, she began to work at the worn place. Scraping away the clay filling and continuing the work that looked as if it had been started by an animal, she enlarged the hole bit by bit. Tossing her cloak in front of it, she hid it with her body when Edmund brought her an evening meal. When night fell, the hole was large enough for her to crawl through. She took her chance before Edmund returned to rest for the night.

Taking off her bulky tunic and with her braid secured inside her veil, she eased her way through, trying to be as quiet as possible. The number of men camping and carousing on the other side of the cottage, obviously in celebration of their coming victories, covered most of the sounds she made.

She stayed low to the ground and used the surrounding trees to hide her movements before reaching her husband and his men. Crouching down behind him, she realised she had no dagger with which to cut his ropes. Trying to untie them proved a waste of time, for the knots held and her fingers could not loosen them.

'I need a knife or something sharp,' she whispered, looking over at the camp and wondering if she could find something there without being detected.

Giles mumbled through the gag and she tugged it free. He began to give her a furious order, but she stopped him with her kiss. Even knowing that danger surrounded them, she took that moment to taste him and to share her love with him. 'I love you, Giles,' she said, kissing him again. 'No matter what happens, do not forget that.'

'There is a dagger in my boot,' he whispered to her, trying to bring his leg closer so she could reach it without stepping from the shelter of the tree he was tied to.

Their armour and weapons had been removed, but Edmund's men had missed the small dagger he always carried there. He waited as she slid her hands down his leg and reached in his boot to take it. The feel of her hands even at the worst of times brought him joy, but for now other matters were more pressing than his ever-present desire for her.

She was sawing through the thick ropes with the dagger when he heard the sound of someone coming through the trees and brush behind them. Fayth gasped and stood away, but he was able to pull free from what she'd done already. Climbing quickly to his feet, he found his wife holding Brice at bay with only the dagger.

''Twould seem that my place at your back has been taken up by someone else,' Brice said.

'It would,' he agreed and he pulled Fayth to him and kissed her while Brice and Lucien freed the other two.

'Do you never obey me, wife? You were supposed to remain in your chambers,' he teased. When her eyes filled with tears, he held her in his embrace for a moment. 'We will settle this when we return to Taerford. I brought something to you.'

He reached inside the gambeson and took out the rings. 'I found these on the floor and knew you would never have left them behind.' She took them and pulled the ribbon loose.

'I have much to answer for, Giles. Much. But know that I did not leave willingly with Edmund.'

Brice came over then, gave them a disgruntled order to move along and handed a mail shirt and sword to Giles. Fayth stood back and watched as he pulled the hauberk over his head and belted it around his waist. 'Not yours, but we came across this on our travels.'

When he looked at Fayth to order her away to

safety, she held out her hand to him. The two rings were in her palm.

'Take this ring as a sign of my fealty to you, Lord Giles,' she whispered. She offered him her father's ring.

At first, he was stunned by her gesture, but then he realised what she was doing and what that ring meant to her. He nodded and held out his hand for her to place the ring on his finger. Knowing what he must do, he took the smaller ring from her and held it before her.

'Take this ring as a sign of my fealty and love, lady,' he said, sliding the ring on her hand as she offered it to him.

He took her by the shoulders and kissed her fiercely. The rest would have to wait. 'Now seek cover near the cottage and do not follow me,' he ordered.

He watched with Brice in stunned silence as she actually made her way to the cottage as he'd ordered her to do, without question or hesitation.

'Mayhap she is learning, my lord?' Brice asked, handing him another dagger.

'Mayhap.' Giles watched as more men poured

from the woods behind them. 'How many did you bring?'

'These are not my men, Giles. These are your lady's men.'

Overwhelmed by the sight of the Saxon knights lined up to fight for their lady, he could only nod. Finally, after acknowledging them, he said, 'Let us go and find Edmund and end this now.'

Chapter Twenty-One

Fayth offered up an oath to the Almighty that if He allowed Giles to live, she would spend her life trying to be the wife he'd dreamed of having. She begged for His protection. And in the end, she just prayed. But from the place where Giles had ordered her, for she would obey him in this.

Fayth watched as her father's men came out of the woods and lined up behind Giles and his men. Together they strode towards the encampment, not bothering to hide their approach. To her surprise, even more followed out of the woods, some nodding to her as they passed. She thought it not possible, but there were some of the peasants that had escaped Lord Huard and others she did not recognise, all following her Norman, Breton, husband into this battle.

Giles did not pause, sighting Edmund and charging forward at him, sword raised, battle cry on his lips.

'Taerford!' he yelled, engaging Edmund alone. To her amazement, the others stood back and waited—for orders or for the outcome, she knew not, but this became a private combat between the two lords.

She cringed at the sound of it, swords clashing, metal screaming as it slid against metal. Memories of their last fight struck her and she could not watch. Turning away, she closed her eyes against the reality that would find her oldest friend or dear husband dead.

The fighting went on and on until suddenly, there was silence. Afraid to discover the results, she waited to hear the screams of the victorious side. Instead she was forced to turn and look across to the camp.

Giles stood over Edmund with his sword pointed at his neck. One movement, one small, easy push, and it was over. Edmund's life. England's last hope. Her friend. Her father's liege lord.

She waited, unable to take a breath or utter a word, for Giles to lean on his sword and bring all this to an end.

* * *

All he had to do was push. He panted now, exhausted by two days with little sleep, little food and only the terror that he had lost Fayth to fill his thoughts. A small thrust and Edmund's threat would be over. Fayth and their lands would be safe from further machinations. William would be rid of another of Harold's kin with a claim to England's throne.

With only one small thrust, it was over.

He looked over at Fayth and at first she did not even look in his direction. Eyes closed, he knew she prayed, but for which one? Then she opened her eyes and he stared at her, knowing now that she would not beg for Edmund's life this time. Having thought of all the possibilities, Giles would rather have been forced to kill him without thinking, for it would leave less guilt in his heart.

He smiled grimly, realising that he'd given Fayth the same choice and asked her to make it. Aye, being forced to something was much easier than choosing on your own. And though now she would not beg for Edmund's life, he would spare it for her and for their future together.

'Take your men and go, Edmund.'

Lifting his sword, he allowed Edmund to climb to his feet. Brice protested loudly, as did his men, but the Saxons who stood at his back were silent.

'Giles, the duke wants him dead,' Brice argued.

'I want him dead, but there are many reasons to let him live,' Giles replied.

'Your grant of lands and title will be in danger if you do this, Giles. Are you certain this is the course you wish to take?' Brice placed his hand on Giles's shoulder and shook him, staring at him as though to make sure he was listening.

Giles paused then, accepting the inherent risks in his plan—the one to aid the runaway serfs and the one to allow Edmund to live yet again.

Turning to Edmund's men, he called out, 'Those who wish to fight with Edmund, take your weapons and go with him. Those who wish peace are welcomed onto my lands.' He spoke to Edmund then, even as Brice grumbled at his side.

'You cannot win this war, Edmund. Even now your boy king seeks terms from William. Morcar and Edwin have deserted his cause, your cause, to protect their own lands in Northumbria. By Christmas, William will be king of England.'

He'd learned much from Bishop Obert before leaving Taerford. The Saxon lords would either submit or die.

'Did you spare my life for her?' Edmund asked, nodding in the direction where Fayth yet stood.

'I did.'

'Did she ask you to do so?'

'Not this time. But I know that killing someone she considered her friend and someone so important to her father would destroy her. I love her and would see her at peace with our life now.'

'This is not the end of it, Norman,' Edmund threatened. 'There are many Saxons who will rally once they know that I lead them.'

Brice growled out a warning, but Giles waved him off.

'Continue this and you will fail, Edmund. And you will take more of your men to their deaths. Accept William and you can all live as free men here,' Giles advised, though he knew the man's answer before any words were spoken.

Edmund shook his head and then looked over to where Fayth yet remained, smiling at her before ordering those following him to pack up the camp. Giles waited until they'd moved off before facing his wife.

Who still stood where he'd ordered her to!

'Do you think she will be more obedient now?' Brice asked, as though reading his thoughts.

'One can only hope, my friend,' he said, clapping him on the shoulder. 'One can only hope.'

And as he signalled her to come to him and they raced to each other, he did have hope. For the first time in his life, he dared to wish for so many things. As he captured her and claimed her before their people, hope and love filled his heart and his arms.

Epilogue

Taerford Manor Keep
Wessex, England
January, 1067

It had taken weeks more to sort out the aftermath of that day, but Bishop Obert proved to be a thoughtful and fair judge of her husband's actions. Of course, Giles's pledge of the current keep and the lands immediately surrounding it for a monastery once they moved further upriver might have smoothed the way. He also had to pledge to help both Brice and Soren when they called upon him to rid the lands of any remaining rebels.

As her husband suspected, the bishop, though serving William, was a pious man of God and welcomed the opportunity that Giles offered.

With his grant expanding the Taerford holdings far past what her father had held, it made sense to locate their new manor house, whatever her Breton husband called it, closer to the new lands and the old.

They spent these short days of winter preparing for the spring when they would finally be able to begin building the keep. He'd even promised her a chamber of her own, for the ladies he said she must have at her side. His friend's wife had written to her, welcoming her as friend and offering the names of two young women who she thought would be amiable companions.

Though accepting the runaways and outlaws onto their land during the winter would be a burden, Giles told the bishop he thought it suitable punishment for failing in his attempt to capture Edmund. If Obert of Caen thought differently, he said not and happily ended his investigation, despite much objection from and stern warnings to Sir Eudes.

Before the bishop left, he'd presented Brice with his grant for lands in Thaxted. There had been trouble there as well, with the old lord's son leading the rebels against King William. Brice would gain the hand of Gillian of Thaxted in marriage, if he could find her and if he could wrestle the keep from her brother. Brice yet remained with them until the winter's snows passed and the roads north opened.

The best news arrived after the bishop returned to London, for it was news that their friend did indeed still live. Giles and Brice often spoke of Soren to Fayth, sharing stories of their misspent youth and bawdy tales she did not need to hear. They believed he might die from his wounds on the battlefield, yet word came of his recovery and his plan to move northward in the spring to claim his lands.

Although they spent the longer nights of winter in pleasurable pursuits, Fayth took time to teach Giles to read and write. His request surprised her, but his determination did not and in only weeks he had progressed beyond both of their expectations.

Now, with the snow covering the lands and much work ahead in the spring, she decided it was time to share her news with her husband.

The stomach ailment she'd suffered the day of

her kidnapping returned again and again and, though not experienced in such matters, it did not take long for her to realise her condition. Emma, who mentioned her courses were late yet again, brought it to her attention. With the number of times her husband had bedded her, it should be no surprise to anyone, but she waited to be certain before revealing it to Giles.

One cold January day, when the winds howled and everyone stayed inside waiting for the storm to pass, Giles ordered her to bed because she looked so pale. It was not such a punishment since he joined her there and when he began exploring her body, touching her and wooing her with his mouth and hands, she discovered she did not feel as poorly as she'd thought. His hands and mouth on her breasts caused a sensitivity she'd not felt before and she wondered if it was due to the babe she carried inside.

When Giles rolled to his side and pulled her into his arms and when they could both breathe again, she took the hand he used to tease her breast and placed it on her belly. There was no sign there yet of her condition, but by winter's end it would show, Emma had told her.

'The spring will be a busy time for us,' she said, watching his face to savour the moment he understood.

'Aye, the new keep should be finished by planting time,' he said. 'Hallam has many plans for the new fields.'

'I think that summer and autumn will prove just as busy, husband,' she began. 'Crops in the field to bring to harvest, preparations for the winter, a babe to care for, men to train...'

She was prepared to continue listing all the tasks ahead, but the expression on his face and the way his hand now touched her belly told her that he understood.

'Truly?' he whispered, spreading his hand wide across her belly. 'Truly?'

'Aye, husband. Emma thinks late August.'

'At harvest time? That is a busy time,' he teased. 'We will keep you working in the fields until the pains are upon you.'

'If you show your lands the same care that you show your wife, I suspect fertility will abound here in Taerford.'

'I like the sound of that, lady wife. I must be diligent in my care.' He leaned over and kissed her then, a tender kiss that spoke of his happiness over the news. 'Have you considered what to name the new lord or lady of Taerford?'

''Tis too early for that, Giles. The birth is months and months away.'

'We will discuss our choice for a boy's name, if we are blessed with a son, but I already know what we will call a daughter if so blessed.'

'You do?' she asked, though she suspected what it might be.

He'd told her over and over how he'd never allowed himself to think that he would ever be more than a bastard knight, riding in service for one lord or another. But something in the words of his friend Simon had spurred him on in his dreams and given him…

'Hope,' they both said at the same time.

He kissed her then, one that spoke of hope and the future and love. And if they stayed abed a few more hours, who would notice such a thing on the dark day of winter?

And so, on the morning of the sixth day of August in the Year of Our Lord 1067, Lady Hope was born in Taerford Keep. But if you asked anyone who lived there, they could tell you that hope came to Taerford the year before, in the guise of a Norman, nay Breton, conqueror.

* * * * *

Author Note

Although the 1066 invasion of Duke William of Normandy brought about huge changes in the politics and society of England, some of those changes were already underway. Normans had become an integral part of England during Edward the Confessor's reign; many gaining lands and titles long before the Conqueror set foot there. So, the Saxons had some experience with Norman ways before this major invasion force landed in Pevensey in October, 1066.

Many Saxons held their lands after William's arrival—those who pledged their loyalty to the new ruler were permitted to retain them, but many were supplanted by those who'd fought for William. Important Norman nobles gained more property and often Saxon heiresses.

Thought ruthless and not hesitant about using force to implement his rule, William did not employ it fully after the Battle of Hastings until the revolt three years later in the north of England. Then, he unleashed his anger on those in what's still called 'the Harrowing of the North', destroying everything in his path and effectively wiping out what was left of the Saxon way of life.

In my story, one of Harold's sons, Edmund, appears as the possible rescuer of Fayth and as a leader of the rebels. 'My' Edmund is really a composite of several real people who lived in the aftermath of the Battle of Hastings and continued to fight the Normans as they moved from the southeast of England northwards and westwards to take control of the whole country. It is believed that at least two of Harold's sons did survive (or avoid) the Battle that killed their father and that they and their mother joined in the efforts of some of the others opposing the Normans. The earls of Mercia and Northumbria, Harold's brothers-by-marriage, switched sides several times during this conflict and were part of this struggle that led to William's Harrowing of the North.

So, any resemblance of Edmund to the real protagonists of history is intentional!